Forbidden Taboo Sex Stories

BDSM, Threesomes, Bisexual, Milfs, Anal Sex, Gangbang, Lesbian and Much More

Rubin Smith

Table of Contents

Elizabeth's House

It was never quite Xavier's intention to make his way to Elizabeth's house as he had done. He had spent the last several weeks going over ideas and plans in his head, though each and every one of them was often stopped with the thought of how ridiculous it all seemed to be. This is it, Xavier thought to himself as he stood in the garden below. Although there was no one around, he couldn't help but feel as if he was being watched. He knew it was possible that he was just anxious, scared, and nervous. He had never done anything quite like this. He didn't know whether to call it an adventure, a risk or both, but one thing was for certain, he had already come so far, and he wasn't turning back.

As he stood in the gardens below, he was able to look up towards the window to the room he knew belonged to Elizabeth. Weeks of planning had also meant driving by her neighborhood, paying attention to her house, and making sure to figure out the right time of day to arrive, and which part of the house she would be most likely to be in. After his research, he quickly learned that it was likely best that he arrived quite late at night after Elizabeth was already in bed.

With slow, steady steps he made his way through the garden scape, approaching the window he knew to belong to Elizabeth's bedroom. He could feel his heart pounding in his chest as he crept forward, careful not to be seen. So close, he thought once more to himself as a shaky breath escaped his lips. He could feel his body trembling lightly with nervous movement as he approached the backside of the house where Elizabeth's bedroom was.

His mind was racing with thoughts of excitement as he approached the wall of the house. After extensive study, he had learned that Elizabeth lived alone, much to his delight. Without another thought, he finally moved forward and grabbed to the lattice against the wall that held up many a garden vine. Gripping it tightly and pushing his foot into one of the many openings. Xavier began to scale the wall, taking each movement very slowly, one step at a time. Lattice diamond by diamond he made his way up towards the window. He could already see that the lights were off and that only the faint glow of a nightlight shone through the window.

As he reached the top of the lattice, he was finally able to heave a sigh of relief. He stayed there for a moment, catching his breath and calming his nerves. Finally, with a deep exhale he leaned forward and peered carefully into the window. He couldn't make out too much through the blinds, but in the dimly lit room, he could see a lump moving beneath a set of blankets. It appeared to be Elizabeth's breathing which made the covers slowly rise and fall, leading him to believe she was likely already asleep.

With careful hands, he reached up and slowly pushed against the window seal. Much to his surprise, it was unlocked. Another wave of relief washed over his body as a grin grew over his face. Pushing upwards he slowly and carefully guided the window upwards, just enough so that he could slowly fit his body inside. He was as quiet as a mouse as he made his way through the window and into the room. He could feel the warmth radiate around him as he entered the four walls, slowly stepping down onto the floor below.

Once inside, he could hear the faint sound of Elizabeth breathing. It was all he could do to remain calm as he slowly turned around and closed the window, making sure that any draft wouldn't wake her. As he slowly approached the bed, he could feel his heart beating faster still. So many weeks of planning, so many years of desire, and it was finally all about to come to a head. Stepping forward he moved so that he could get a better look at Elizabeth in her bed. Just as he had hoped she was laying there asleep, her beautiful face illuminated by the soft lighting in the room. For a moment all he did was stand there and look at her, watching the movement of her body rise and fall with every breath.

He thought for a moment about turning around, walking away, and pretending it had never happened, but he was already so close. Closing his eyes, he felt a wave of cool air take over him. It was all at once when his body disbanded from a solid-state, into that of something more supernatural. With a silent poof, he felt himself shift into a state of ghostly apparition. Thrusting himself forward took into the air and leaped forward, aiming himself towards the sleeping body of Elizabeth.

Before he knew it, he felt a shock of cold followed by the sensation of warm body heat. Opening his eyes, he suddenly felt himself laying comfortably in Elizabeth's bed. It was even more comfortable than he imagined as he slowly rolled over. Now inside of Elizabeth's body, he was able to control all of her movements. She was completely lost for consciousness and control as Xavier laid there, reveling in the sensation.

"I can't believe this," Xavier finally spoke out loud, his voice still very much his own. His own glowing eyes peered around the room as he slowly sat up and looked down at Elizabeth's magnificent body. It was everything he knew it was, and more. As he looked down, he could see the beautiful mounds of her two curvy breasts right before his eyes, a silk nightgown draped gingerly over top of them. Her flat, strong stomach held her core upright, and the thin, white nightgown rode up to the top of her thighs revealing her beautiful skin underneath.

Xavier's hands tingled with anticipation as he slowly reached down and gently cupped at her breasts. He could feel their soft, mailable texture as he squeezed them lightly. Her nipples were already hardening, likely from his own arousal. He could see them slowly begin to protrude and point outwards, becoming visible through the thin nightgown. With careful movements he reached down and slowly began to squeeze at the nipples, prodding, pulling, and twisting them softly. The pleasure radiated through his body unlike anything else head ever experienced. All he wanted was to enjoy himself and feel the type of things he had never felt before.

After a moment he slowly rose up from the bed. As his feet reached the floor, he looked down once more to examine Elizabeth's standing body. He lightly twisted from side to side, making her nightgown twist and turn with him. Something about the feeling of the silk on her legs made him tingle in a way he had never experienced. An audible sigh escaped Elizabeth's lips as Xavier curled them into a smile. Stepping forward, he made his way over to a full-length mirror for a better look. His first instinct was to rip off the gown and see what was underneath, but he knew there were better ways.

His eyes peered around the room curiously before finding landing on the door of her closet. He stepped forward, Elizabeth's beautiful petite feet slapping lightly against the hardwood floor. He could still feel the nervous tension in the air as he reached forward and opened the closet door, curious to see what was inside. As he reached out to turn on the light, he was overwhelmed to see a walk-in closet, six or seven times the size of his own. Each side of the closet was lined with clothes from end to end. He was overwhelmed and amazed all at once as he looked around, wanting to get a better look at some of the outfits.

Slowly and carefully he began to sort through every item in the closet, curious to see what he could find. He worked for nearly half an hour putting together outfits and combinations, interested in trying something on to delight himself. Taking a deep breath, he closed his eyes. He didn't want to see Elizabeth completely naked until he felt the time was right, so as he undressed her body from the nightgown, he kept his eyes peering away, to keep from seeing what he was trying to save for later.

Slowly he began to dress himself, curious to see what he could put together. First, he worked out an outfit that thrilled him in particular. A clean white shirt and black school girl styled skirt seemed like a great outfit for the first time. It took him a little while to figure out exactly how to put it on. He was so used to the typical jeans and tees, that all the buttons and the fasteners for the women's clothes did seem a little daunting at first. He did his best to keep his eyes cast away or closed, refusing to take in the sight of her naked body too soon.

First, he worked the white shirt over her head, pulling it down. Lifting her arms, he grasped at her hair and pulled it out from where it was tucked in the shirt collar. He could feel the silky soft strands of her hair running through her fingertips. He could smell the lingering scent of her floral and citrus shampoo in her nose as her hair wafted around before falling down over her back and shoulders. Then he took up the black skirt and opened up the waistband. Moving carefully, trying not to look he stepped down into the skirt before finally pulling it up and over her waist. The freedom he felt was almost indescribable as he finally looked down. He couldn't see much of the outfit, so he turned and made his way back into her room to take a look into the mirror. As he walked, he enjoyed seeing her skirt flair out, twist, and turn with every step he took.

"Holy Cow," he spoke aloud as he turned and looked in the mirror. Everything about the outfit as exactly as he pictured, bringing him great happiness. As he looked at her in the mirror, he could still see her hardened nipples poking out through the fabric of the white top. For the moment though his eyes were pulled down further, once more to her beautiful, glistening thighs. The black, school girl styled skirt was quite short indeed, giving him all of the more leg to be able to look at. What he enjoyed most about the outfit was not only had subtly sexy it was, but also the simplicity. Standing there in the mirror, looking at her body, he felt sexy, beautiful, but even more important comfortable. Sighing lightly, he reached up and grasped hold of her hips and gave them a firm squeeze. He couldn't help but shake her hips side to side and watch as her skirt moved alongside her body. Everything about the outfit was perfect, but he wanted to see more.

He didn't want to see her naked yet, he didn't want to ruin the surprise, but he did want to see more. Moving back towards the closet he slowly removed the clothes, once more keeping his eyes cast away from her body as he walked. He took care to remove the shirt and skirt as carefully as possible and hang them back up in the exact same manner they had been hung up before, and in the exact same spot. The next thing to meet his eye was yet again another skirt, but one much different than the last he had tried on. This one was a little rougher around the edges, made of an almost denim material, but black in color. Strings of loose thread hung unraveled at the hemline, giving it a sexier appeal, and a little bit edgier style.

For the top, Xavier was quick to choose a gray, crop top with almost a sweater-like feel. Just something about picking and choosing clothes to go on Elizabeth's body turned him on unlike he had ever thought possible. He could feel Elizabeth getting wetter by the moment due to his arousal. He was sure that if he had put panties on her, they would had already been drenched with juices. Finally finishing up with the next outfit, he strutted back into her room, letting her body move just as sexy and confident as ever. As he took his place once more in front of her mirror, he took a slow, subtle, deep breath and opened his eyes once more, looking down with excitement towards the mirror.

Somehow this look turned him on even more. He could hardly hold in his excitement as he opened his eyes to look at it. He was right in thinking the denim skirt was sexier with its harsher fabric and stray sprigs of thread and twine. The crop top showed off just a bit of her navel as well which he loved, giving him just a little bit more insight into how Elizabeth's body must look beneath her clothes. Reaching her hand down he grasped lightly at her belly, rubbing her fingertips along her soft skin. He could tell that she worked out, as he was able to feel the light ripple of her muscles beneath her soft, feminine stomach. He curled her toes once more with anticipation as he let the tension build up even more in his body.

Taking a deep breath, he stepped closer to the mirror. He started to walk in place, taking steps and watching how her breasts bounced. Without a bra underneath her breasts moved freely under the sweater like crop top. He enjoyed watching how they bounced up and down beneath the shirt, but what he loved, even more, was the sensation of her nipples rubbing against the fabric with each bounce. Once more he could feel the wetness growing heavier as he resisted the urge to lay down and masturbate right then and there. He knew that if he built himself up a little more with excitement then when it came time for the big one, he would be happier that he waited.

He turned and looked one more time at the outfit before turning and heading back to the closet. The skirts and shirts were nice, but he wanted something sexier, even more feminine, so as he made his way into the closet, he immediately shifted his attention towards there dresses. There were probably a hundred ore more hanging there, all of varying colors, shapes, and sizes. He could only imagine how each one must look on her tall, lean, body. He wondered if she had worn them all before as he sorted through the dresses picking out his favorites.

The first one he picked up was one of many all black numbers. Lifting it up he was able to see its unique shape. It had off the shoulder sleeves and an A line hang which quickly drew his eye. He didn't know that much about clothes, but he was able to tell what would look good on a woman's body, so without another moment's hesitation he quickly slid the dress on. It took him a few minutes to get the zipper pulled up and closed on her back, but when he did, he wasted no time turning around and quickly shuffling her feet forward back to the mirror.

He felt her breath leave her body this time as he looked at her in the mirror. She was stunning, gorgeous, beautiful, sexy, even more so than he had ever thought before. This dress was perfect, utterly perfect. Looking at it he wondered if he would even be able to find anything else that fit her body as well as this did. He took up he hands and began to run them down over her hips and outer thighs. The way the dress accentuated her every curve made him practically melt. His eyes fluttered with excitement

The sleek black nature of the dress was perfect, and the way her hair hung over top of her shoulders and breasts just contrasted beautifully with the colors. He had never seen something so sexy, felt so turned on, or so absolutely thrilled. Reaching up he fondled at her breasts once more, shifting her body so that her knees were drawn together. He knew right then he wanted more, and so once again he rushed back in the closet, in search for something even more daring.

He searched once more for outfit after outfit until he came across a second dress, with a similar appeal. This one too seemed to be body-hugging, and somewhat revealing, so without a second question, he quickly removed the black dress, hanging it back up and donned himself in another dress, a sparkling silver one, that he couldn't wait to see.

Looking at her body in the mirror once more, he couldn't help but feel somewhat glamorous. This was obviously the type of dress she would wear to an important event. The off the shoulder top of the dress provided a sneak peek to her skin, showing off her delicate collar bone. The long flowy nature of the dress was beautiful, but the side split up the leg gave it a certain sexy quality that he simply wasn't' ready for. However, something about the dress just wasn't quite what he was looking for. He wanted something more, more flowy, less glitzy, something classic and beautiful.

Twisting her lips to the side he quickly turned and made his way back into the closet for one more attempt at finding the perfect dress. He liked the color of the silver, and the length, but something about it just wasn't right, but then he saw it. The dress he knew was going to be the perfect fit. Opening his eyes wide he dashed her body forward and grabbed a hold of it, stripping himself from the other dress quickly and haphazardly. With a little bit of shimmy and shaking, he got into the new dress and right away he could tell it was the one he had been looking for.

"This is it!" he gasped out loud. "This is the one!" He felt like a goddess looking at her body wearing the dress. It had a Greek appeal, long, and draped, white, and sleek. It was almost sheer down towards the bottom giving him the perfect view of her well-toned legs. Everything about it was simply perfect. This time he looked into the mirror for a long time taking in the sight of the dress. He was sure that if he left it on too long the thin fabric of it would start to take on the moisture that had accumulated in her groin, so he headed towards the closet one more time.

I think I'm ready for something more, he thought to himself as his eyes wandered over to her sportswear section. In the section, there was everything from yoga pants, sports bras, leotards, and bikinis. Suddenly a brilliant idea met his mind. Picking up several things he was overwhelmed with excitement as he found himself liking the idea of doing a little striptease. So, with great excitement, he layered some of the clothes together, a pair of yoga pants and a sports bra over top of a bikini. The sports bra and pants kept the fabric of the bikini hidden just enough so that he could do his own striptease and surprise himself in front of the mirror.

This time he ran to the mirror even faster than before, so excited he could barely contain himself. First, he looked at himself in the yoga pants and sports bra. Just like he thought her abdomen was very well toned. He felt as if he had no words as he looked at all of the skin showing beneath her clothes. Turning to the side he took a moment to gander at her ass in the yoga pants. A smirk grew over her face as he reached her hand down and squeezed firmly to her ass before slapping it lightly. A light chuckle escaped his lips as he turned back to the mirror, anxious to see what was beneath the work out gear. He wasted little time, ripping off the workout gear to get to the bikini. He knew it was going to be the most revealing yet and he could hardly wait.

The bright yellow material of the bikini caught his eye in stark contrast to the dark yoga pants and sports bra. As he peeled away the pants and bra he felt Elizabeth's heart skip a beat, in reaction to his excitement. He shook her hips and moved her body as if music was playing, as he stripped away the sports gear to reveal the full bikini. It was unlike anything he had ever seen. Her entire body minus a few important parts were on full display for him and he could hardly contain his excitement, that was until he felt himself start to be pulled away.

For some reason, his connection to Elizabeth was growing weaker. He had never possessed someone's body for so long, and he felt sure that was why it was happening. He knew he had to get her to the bed and quick, so he turned on her heel and quickly run and dove into the bed, doing his best to lay her down and wrap her up. No sooner than he lifted the cover with her hand did he feel himself pushed out of her.

"Huh? What's going on?" suddenly came Elizabeth's voice, mumbling lightly. Xavier's apparitional state quickly hid in the shadows of the room as he peered over at Elizabeth for a moment. He watched as she shifted in the bed, slowly sitting up and looking around, surprised and confused. Her breathing was heavy and sharp, indicating she was scared and confused. As her eyes journey from wall to wall, she slowly began to feel the cool air on her body, causing her to look down.

"What the – "she started to say, shocked to find herself no longer wearing her favorite gown, but instead the revealing, brightly colored bikini. Her legs shot out from underneath her as she tried to get off the bed. Xavier peered over to the floor in front of the mirror where he had peeled away the work out clothes. They were still laying there in a pile and he had to be sure she didn't find them. Suddenly with another burst forward, he held his breath and shot towards her body. Just like before Elizabeth never saw it coming

All at once Xavier pushed his way back into her body, stiffening it like a board. As if on queue the brightness of his own eyes glowed, almost superimposed over her own. He took fast, staggered breath with Elizabeth's lungs as he looked around in a panic, feeling her body start to go limp as she faded back into unconsciousness. Woah, he thought to himself as he moved once again to keep her upright. There we go.

It took a few minutes for him to regain his composure, but he was quick to get back to trying on clothes. He had, had his sights set on two more outfits, the most exciting of all of the categories, lingerie. So back into the closet, he went, emerging firstly in a set of red lingerie, nearly as bright to the eye as the bikini. As he stood in front of the mirror, he felt himself overwhelmed. He knew if he had been in his own body, he'd have an erection unlike any other right now as he stared at Elizabeth's body in the revealing set.

Once more the breath left his body. The sexy lingerie, coupled with the exhilaration of Elizabeth waking up, and everything else that had happened overwhelmed him to the fullest. Looking at her now he knew that he was almost to the point he could barely take another moment of holding off. He wanted to try on just one more outfit, more lingerie, and the sexiest thing he found in her closet. He had it set in his mind that he would put on the lingerie, and then watch himself peel it off her body. Then he would finally see her naked for the first time and get exactly what he wanted. So, with that, he headed into the closet for the very last time.

As his eyes opened in front of the mirrors for the last time, he was completely overwhelmed by what he saw. This lingerie wasn't a simple set of bras and panties, or just a lace thong or cover-up. It was beautiful, sexy, classy, and even glamorous. It looked expensive, it was comfortable, and most of all it adorned her body, unlike anything he had seen so far. In short, it was stunning.

It had everything. A beautiful light gray bra with fancy lace details. A matching g string that hugged and curved her hips and thighs perfectly. A breast-baring top net cover that accentuated her breasts, pushing them together and lifting them perfectly into the bra. An embroidered lace detailing on the net that wrapped around her lower body, extending past her stomach and even moving down her legs. Finally, he had found the perfect outfit, the thing he had been looking for since the start and he couldn't be happier.

As he lifted her arms up once more, he rubbed over her breasts one last time. He could feel that her body saw so wet, so excited that he couldn't wait a minute longer. Reaching up he slowly began to remove the clothes, swaying lightly like a striptease. Bit by bit peeled away from her skin, exposing her perfect body. Her round beautiful breasts, with hardened pink nipples. Her sexy, toned belly, and curvy hips, and finally, her soft, delicate pussy. Everything had fallen right into place, and finally Xavier was able to sit there and look in the mirror, admiring Elizabeth's fully nude body for the very first time.

He could not take second more as he reached down and slowly rubbed her fingers between the slit of her wet pussy. He could feel her clitoris swollen with arousal as he rubbed her fingers over it. He wasted no time getting to the floor so he could watch himself delight her body and his own mind. The pleasure was unlike anything he had ever experienced as he began to rub faster. Her long, slender arms were able to reach everything perfectly allowing for him to slowly begin to slip fingers inside of her.

All at once he was thrusting slowly in and out of her, rubbing her thumb against her clitoris, and pinching at her pink, delicate nipples. The pleasure overwhelmed him like something he never thought possible as he quickly found his body quivering and trembling in delight. Each thrust of the fingers was long and slow at first, moving in such a way that he could feel every inch of them as they pushed in and out of her. Slowly he began to pick up speed and add more fingers until three of them were pushing inside of her all at once.

As he pumped in and out of her, he used her thumb to focus on her clitoris. He wanted to feel it all at once, he wanted it to end a final explosion that he would never forget. He couldn't help but moan as he arched her back and let her lean against the bed. He was already fully panting, having been so turned on he was already near climax. She was so wet that it took little effort to thrust the fingers up and down rapidly. He could feel the sensation of her uterus contracting with pleasure with each and every thrust as she quickly grew closer and closer to orgasm.

His fingers pinched, pulled, and prodded at her nipples as he slowly leaned back further, laying down to the floor and turning to the side so he could watch himself in the mirror. He watched as her body wiggled and writhed in delight as he stroked against her. He was gasping, moaning, and groaning as he felt a heat rise to her head as she drew closer and closer to the peak of pleasure. Everything slowly hazed and fogged around him as his eyes zoomed into the mirror fixating only on his hand stroking her clitoris and pumping in and out of her.

He could feel her breasts bouncing up and down with every thrust. He could feel her own juices rolling over her fingers and thighs, making a little puddle on the floor where she was laying. All he could do was hold her breath as he felt the tension in her body grow to an all-time high. He pumped harder, faster, and stronger. He flicked her clitoris faster, and faster, rounding it and moving back and forth. He pulled on her nipples, squeezing her breasts and taking in the sensation of her soft delicate skin beneath her own finger tips.

Then suddenly he felt the absolute strong sensation he had ever felt in his life. Her uterus contracted hard and all of the tension in her body began to release. It moved up towards her head then back down to her toes before pulsing in her groin and radiating outwards. All at once he began to orgasm inside of her body, the most vibrant and strongest orgasm that he had ever experienced. He couldn't move or breath, he just sat there struggling to keep thrusting as he felt the tightness of her pussy squeeze around her fingers, the squeezing lingering for the many seconds the orgasms lasted until finally he felt a sudden high and fell back to the floor, out of breath, tingling, and overwhelmed with sensation.

As he lay on the floor all he could do was focus on his breathing. His eyes were closed, he wasn't listening, he was just laying there reveling in the remnants of the pleasure as it slowly started to fade. My God, he thought to himself as he turned over once more to peer into the mirror across from him. Finally, with a slow deep breath, he slowly guided his hand back towards her clitoris, a devilish smile appearing one last time over her face. "Okay," he spoke out loud, sighing with delight. "Time for round two."

Try a Threesome

"I'd like to try a threesome!" My wife's simple unsolicited one-liner about what had been an uneventful dinner at home up until that point caused quite a stir to say the least. Admittedly, as many husbands fantasize about it, I have been making this suggestion for years - and have been turned down with great hostility; so what happened? Was it something she had read, seen on television or in the cinema, or was it just a random thought that seemed fascinating? Honestly, I didn't care - if she was ready for it, so was I!!

Now the basic rules. After a series of lengthy discussions, we decided to have two independent events: a male-female-male and a male-female male-female. Each conversation was exciting and the anticipation was overwhelming. Oh dear, I was walking around half-erect all the time, and my wife was much more attentive in bed. Even if nothing more happened, it was already stimulating to just talk about it!

Before we present our game plan, let me describe both my wife and me. I am six feet tall, weigh 170 pounds, have brown eyes, black thinning hair, a 6-inch penis that is quite thick, and instead of having a six-pack for abs, my wife teases me by saying I have a one-pack. I have been an athlete all my life and have spent a reasonable amount of time at the gym. I am over 60 years old, but I don't look and act like one. Most people find me approachable, funny and "well-groomed".

My wife is gorgeously dead! She is 5'6" tall, weighs 110 pounds, has brown almond shaped eyes, reddish brown streaked hair, a sweet upturned nose, a great round and firm butt, fantastic thighs, hips and calves, perfect lips, silky skin and natural 34 Ds to die for. She also has a beautifully groomed pubic area with a pile of black pubic hair and is shaved from vagina to anus. She's younger than me and literally looks like she's in her 40s! We've been married since early college.

Once that was out of the way, the question arose as to where we would find willing partners. We thought of all sorts of places, but chose the most logical one - the gym. We both trained several times a week for several years and during this time we both found a number of friends and acquaintances. We decided to change our normal daily routine and to change and shower before and after each training session, still in the gym instead of at home. This would keep us with our friends a little longer and allow us to examine the "goods" more closely.

My wife determined what she would like a male partner to do, just as I did with the woman. The next week I spent time examining the 4 or 5 friends of mine that came into question. In the end I chose David for several reasons, he is: mid to late 40s, divorced, taller than me, very well built, has a solid ass and abs and has a very impressive "uncut" penis. In addition, David has made subtle remarks to me over the years about how beautiful my wife is and how lucky I am to be with her.

I turned to David and asked him if we could have a highly confidential conversation. When he agreed, I explained what we would ask of him, that this was a "one and done" and that there were no conditions. After assuring himself that I was serious, he declared his willingness to participate.

My wife had a similar experience in her dressing room. She approached both a blonde and a dark-haired woman - both beautiful and seductive. Both met my criteria: excellent body, fabulous face and lips, no tattoos or piercings, naturally large breasts and areolas and a well cared for vagina. When she pointed this out to me, I decided to go for the dark-haired beauty - her name is Gabrielle, or Gabby for my wife.

My wife turned to Gabby, also in confidence, explained the same basic rules only once and pointed me to Gabby after the conversation so she could look at me. She liked what she saw and she agreed - our selection was now complete and on board.

The next phase of preparation was to figure out how we could do this. We came to the conclusion that there would be two different scenarios and that the male-female would be the first. We did this because we thought it was possible that David would not be as gentle as Gabby and that there might be some after-effects

- like a sore pussy. So Gabby was invited to our home for a pleasant, relaxed evening, and later in the month David would join us in our dark, discreet and remote Italian trattoria.

The week's wait for the evening with Gabby seemed to go on forever. The anticipation for both my wife and me was really fun. We went through a series of scenarios, which in the end didn't matter because everything went smoothly. At 6pm Gabby arrived in a sun dress with spaghetti straps exposing her tanned shoulders and a pair of flat trousers. She looked beautiful. My wife was wearing black pants with a modestly low-cut white blouse and no bra. Me, khakis and a polo shirt.

My wife served hors d'oeuvres and we all started drinking a very good champagne while we got to know each other better. This lasted almost half an hour, then dinner was served together with more wine. As hoped, the wine began to work on both women, and the conversation revolved around sex and the reason why we were all together. More wine, and that was all that was needed. When my wife bent down to serve Gaby, she (Gaby) looked down at my wife's blouse, stretched her hand upwards, gently took my wife's neck and pulled it down to give her a soft, erotic and passionate kiss - with tongue. This was exactly the way my wife and I had hoped it would start. We quickly went into the bedroom.

My wife made an excellent choice! Gabby is 50 years old, widowed for several years and has two teenage daughters living at home. She is six feet tall, weighs 120 pounds, has black hair, purple eyes and very fair skin. Like my wife, she has natural breasts, a C-cup, with large nipples that, when aroused, are pointed and straight outwards; very swollen pussy lips; she is firm and well-groomed - a product of a lot of yoga; and she has a bikini cut, which unfortunately for me has only left a "catwalk" of pubic hair (I like a bushier pussy). Shortly after going to bed we discovered that Gaby's most unusual body part is her clitoris: it is huge - much bigger than my wife. With no hair in that area, her clitoris is fully accessible and when she is aroused, incredibly sensitive. My wife and I were amazed and envious of her size and took turns touching, licking and sucking her. This was, I confess, a beautiful thing and a wonderful surprise!

Gabby and my wife undressed each other, then they both undressed me and led me to the bed. I was trapped between two beautiful women - unbelievable. The kissing and body contact started immediately. I had never had another woman since my marriage, and my wife had never been touched - let alone kissed - by another woman: This experience left us breathless at first. It was intoxicating. The girls kissed and touched each other's ears, neck, tits, pussy, ass and clitoris, while somehow they also paid a lot of attention to my body and penis. I can only describe the lovemaking of these two mature women as "refined" and very sensual. I paid that little bit to be the necessary man!

The first orgasm came quite quickly for each of us, then we engaged in a few wonderful hours of loving, touching, exploring, intercourse, cunnilingus and enjoying. The women all had multiple orgasms that seemed to never end and I had 3. Around 1am we all showered together, got dressed and said good night. My wife and I agreed that this was even better than we could have imagined and we had another experience to look forward to.

After our first three-way conversation, our anticipation was heightened by the thought of the upcoming night with David. We met, as was fitting, at Amore's at 7 pm and went straight to our table. Speaking of fun: What I didn't know about this man was that he was both an excellent storyteller and had a wonderful sense of humor. We sat, drank, talked, drank some more and never mentioned why we were together. It was like an evening with a great, longtime friend.

After dinner my wife apologized to go to the bathroom and when she came back she leaned over the table and whispered so loudly that we could both hear that she wanted to go home. Then she told David that she had been watching him all night, looking forward to the rest of the evening, and that when she went into the ladies' room, she took off her panties because they were soaked and now the pussy juice was dripping down her leg!

That's all we wanted to hear! I paid the bill immediately and we all jumped into my car with my wife between the two men. Out of the corner of my eye I saw my wife take David's hand and let him stroke the inside of her silky smooth right thigh. She started moaning slightly, pulled up her skirt and let David stick his finger into her pussy - there was a conspicuous slurping sound and a wonderful smell that filled the car. I also noticed that my wife had reached over and rubbed against David's cock and squeezed it through his pants. My erection was palpable!

Once inside, my wife took total control. After she had asked us both to take off our clothes, she wanted David to stand behind her, unbutton her blouse and take off her bra without taking her breasts out of their cups, she just wanted the straps off her shoulders and her arms free. She asked me to kneel down before her, open her skirt, take off her shoes and gently kiss her clitoris while David cupped her breasts and let his erection rest in her ass crack. David and I did what she had been told to do.

Then my wife took a few steps to the side and turned back to us so that she was completely exposed and could watch the two men in front of her. What she saw must have pleased her, because the smile that fell on her face was something I had never seen before! David smiled as well. He and I were both standing in front of my naked wife with erections that could not get any bigger. We were all ready!

Our king-size bed offered just enough room for all of us to enjoy the evening. Since neither David nor I are bi, we both concentrated 100% on my wife. She was amazed at David's cock - it was a good 10 cm longer than mine, almost as thick and had a full hood, something she had never seen before even in pictures. What we did not do to her and she did not do to us!

We kissed, fucked and licked alternately her pussy and clitoris, also her anus, her toes, her wonderful tits, fingers, hands, ears, her neck. My wife screamed, squirmed and begged for more - we stroked her tits, face, hair and pussy - she had sperm dripping all over her body. It wasn't just sex, it was lust and it was intense.

She didn't miss most of our bodies either! My wife has a great head, and she demonstrated all her talents, she kissed and licked us all over our bodies, because she couldn't get enough of us or of her. She was so aroused that it felt like her mouth was literally devouring our faces and tails! I could only imagine it would be like this in an orgy. When I had an orgasm, she immediately turned to David to involve him and vice versa, while all the time she was having orgasms one after the other. Words cannot describe the evening - it was incredible, and my wife was incredible.

Like Gabby, when we were all used up, we showered together and my wife gave us both one last soapy hand job. Afterwards she fell into bed and fell asleep immediately; I took David home and thanked him. He asked when we could do it again, and after reminding him that it was a one-time occurrence, he said he was disappointed but understood.

Over the next few days, weeks, and months, my wife and I discussed the experiences at length as we relived our time with both David and Gabby. Our conclusion, which seems to change with every little nuance we remember, is that at the time of this writing, the evening with David was the winner - two cocks for my wife is much better than one. Apart from that our time with Gabby was unforgettable! Today I am not convinced that this will be our only "One and Done"!

The Horny Club

Chapter 1:

I am Mark and I am addicted to sm. Yet it started very innocently with a classmate (Emily) in high school. One afternoon when I was at her house doing homework together, I accidentally bumped a vase and it fell to the ground. I actually deserve a pack for the buttocks, I said. You are right, come here and she put me down on her knees. She rolled up my skirt and rolled down my pants. I got a few big slaps on my butt and it felt wonderful and exciting. Harder, she asked. I nodded and she pelted even harder. My buttocks were completely red.

From now on, it was hit every time. Every time we found an excuse to give each other a beating. Emily once came up with the news. She had taken a belt from her father. I had to take off my pants and kneel on her bed. She folded the belt in half and gave me a big blow to my buttocks. That hurt, but I didn't want to let me know and asked her for more.

Now the gate was off the dam and I was beaten mercilessly for the first time. I begged her to stop but first got an extra hard blow. Go and stand, then I can see the result you turn around. They look very beautiful red. If you turn around again, I can see your pussy and put on your pants again. The next time it was her turn. I not only wanted to give her a big beating but also humiliate her. I told her in an imperative tone that she had to undress completely. She struggled at first, but when I made it clear to her that I was serious, she pulled everything out until she was completely naked. I looked at her from all sides and felt her breasts and squeezed her nipples and my hand slid down to her pussy. Bend down as much as possible and grab your ankles with your hands. Her buttocks were now tight. I grabbed the belt and started beating her ass hard. She screamed and wanted to come up. I bend over and she obeyed. You get ten more strokes and I want you to name the number after each stroke and ask for the next one. After the ten strokes, I gave her permission to get dressed again.

From that moment on, it was striking and increasingly violent. The next time I was not only beaten with a belt but with a sweeping stick. I was also hit on the back with a whip. It came to an end when her father got another job in Germany and they moved. The last time was horrible and the height of humiliation. I had to lie down on my back on a table and raise and spread my knees. With a wooden spoon with which you normally stir the soup, she hit me on my pussy ten times. I screamed it out. When she finally stopped, she first took a picture of my pussy as a memento. Then I turned the roles around and hit her so hard on her pussy that she couldn't forget me in the first few weeks and took several photos of her naked body. Every time I look at the photos, I still long for her.

But now I have a boyfriend with whom I have wonderful sex every time I come to his room. But I also wanted him to humiliate and hit me. That is why I dropped a plate from my hands in a so-called accident that fell to pieces on the floor. I'm sorry and actually, I deserve a beating on my bare buttocks. He kicked in and said, come here. He loosened my jeans and fastened my jeans and my panties. He put me on his knees and started to give me a lot of beating. Then he put me in bed and took me to his dogs. I said it's your turn next time. I'm curious, he said, smiling. The first next time I came to see him; he laughed a bit because I ruthlessly beat him up. Yet he has the taste.

Just like with Emily, we went further and further. We visited a sex shop and bought all kinds of things such as whips, quirt, slats, handcuffs, ropes, etc.

Now it was 'party' every time.

How nice it would be to beat each other off with a group, I suggested once and do partner exchanges like this.

At a subsequent visit to the sex shop, we talked about it with the owner. He gave us a telephone number of an exclusive sex club that specializes in BDSM.

We called and requested further information. It clicked so well and we made an appointment that he would visit us to see if we belonged to their target group to avoid mutual disappointment. His visit was successful and we received a brochure with rules of conduct such as dress codes, shaved pussy and dick, etc. He invited us for an introduction evening.

On the indicated day, we went to the specified address. It turned out to be a detached farmhouse that had been converted into a clubhouse.

On arrival, we were introduced to the members who were present that evening. It turned out to be six couples from around 18 to 45 years old. One of the men explained how things would go that night. The women would be taken to one of the rooms and blindfolded there.

Then the men went to draw lots with notes with a room number. If you happen to exchange the number of your own partner's room, you could exchange it, but you didn't have to. Some men wanted to redeem their own partners anonymously because the men were not allowed to show who they were. Before I was blindfolded, I could see what was in the room. For example, there was a cross in the shape of the letter X with all kinds of rings.

I was a little nervous, waiting for the man to whom I would be delivered. The door opened and someone approached me. He started to undress me slowly. When I was completely naked, my whole body was felt and touched and especially my breasts and especially my nipples were treated. My pussy was also caught. I got ties around my wrists and ankles. He pushed me forward and tied a rope around my wrist bands. My hands were pulled up. My legs were spread and the straps around my ankles were attached to something. Before I knew it, the first whip hit my back. I screamed it out. Another hard blow and again, I roared. I got something stuffed in my mouth now, probably my panties. One stroke followed the other and my back and buttocks got the full layer. My thighs also got their portion. Suddenly I felt that he hit me now between my legs so that he hit my pussy. I writhed in pain.

Before I knew it, he was on the other side and I was tackled with a quirt from the front. My breasts got the full layer and my nipples were tackled extra with a thin bar. Slowly he went down to my stomach and thighs. Especially the inside of my thighs had his preference. He also hit hard on my pussy with quirt. He finally stopped and released me. He forced me to my knees and he put his dick in my mouth. I had to blow him.

In the end, he pushed me down and pushed his dick into my pussy. He took me hard and squirted his sperm in my pussy. He went out of the door and I took off the blindfold and got dressed.

I went back to the bar. Every woman who returned came with applause.

I thought the idea of not knowing by which man I was beaten and used was terrible. Every guy I looked at said well, you were great. I enjoyed it and thank you. I'd like you to have it every night. My humiliation was complete.

Back in the car, we had a beating fight. I was disgusted by his stories of how he had mercilessly assaulted a 50-year-old fat woman and took it while she begged for mercy.

I've never seen him.

Chapter 2:

After the story of my experiences with SM with Emily and my boyfriend, which I gave the voucher, it now follows how I continued.

I had had enough of the hassle with men for now.

One day the brochure of the sex club came back and was pleased to see that once a month there was a women's evening, where the attention was more focused on pampering each other in groups and less on hard work. Registration in advance was required.

I called to sign up and I could come to the next women's evening.

On the evening in question, I volunteered and was introduced to 8 women of different ages. I estimated from 20 to 50 years. I recognized a woman from the previous evening.

Because I was new, I immediately got full attention. They sat down in a circle. I had to take a seat in the middle. I had to answer all kinds of questions about my sex life.

After this, they slowly asked me to undress completely. I took off my blouse and loosened my bra. They loudly expressed their admiration for my firm's full breasts. Now I opened the closure of my jeans and pulled it off. I was now looking at my panties. They called out pants. I obeyed their demand and rolled down my pants. I stood there completely naked for them. Hands-on your head so that we can take a good look at you. Some came to see me up close. I had to sit down again and answer the question of how much I spoiled myself. On average, once a day, preferably while watching a sex video in which one woman seized the other. Sink a little and spread your legs and show how you spoil yourself.

I hesitated but was told that disobedience would be punished ten strokes with the cane. I started to caress my breasts and turned around my nipples so that they became swollen and hard. Now one hand went down to my pussy and started to grope with fingers. I also went into my pussy with my finger and made sewing movements. I moaned. When they had had enough of seeing me spoiled, I had to stop. The chair was removed and a table replaced it. I had to lie on my back on the table. My hands were tied with ropes to rings on the side of the table. My legs were spread and tied in the same way.

I was completely at the mercy of them and they could celebrate their lusts on me.

Four women approached and started to feel me and especially my breasts and pussy were taken care of. Fingers went into my pussy. First one, then two and more until one woman smeared her hand with oil and slowly entered my pussy and gradually entered deeper. Do you have experience with fisting, they asked. No and I don't want it either. You do not know what you are missing, so we continue. The whole hand was now in my pussy and it hurt first, but gradually the pain diminished again. She moved her hand in my pussy and it felt nice. I had learned something again. Next time we're going to fist in your ass. A woman came walking with all kinds of attributes such as dildos, vibrators, nipple clamps and a device that they would use to milk me.

Four women left to spoil each other in one of the rooms and who knows what else.

I was loosened and now had to get bent on my knees and hands on the table. My hands were tied again. My legs were spread and tied again. Two started to milk me and the other two started to work on my pussy with dildos and vibrators. The two women put glass tubes on my nipples and put pumps on end, sucking the air out of the tubes and sucking in my nipples. With a box connected to the tubes, they could make the sucking go a little softer and then harder again so that my nipples felt like they were being milked, especially because the intake and suction were different per nipple. I felt I was going to come by that they now a dildo in my pussy went back and forth that looked like a real dick. In the meantime, my clit was treated with a vibrator.

I started to shake and it went on all over my body. I felt it in my nipples. I had never come so violently ready.

I was released again and now went with two women to a room where there was a double bed. I had to undress them piece by piece. Now they knelt on the edge of the bed with their buttocks ready to be machined. I grabbed a long thin bamboo cane and, in turn, gave each woman a blow. Because they hardly responded, I started to hit harder and harder.

That had the desired effect because they started screaming in pain and begging for mercy.

I had had enough of it for a while and we got dressed and went back to the bar for a well-earned drink and to chat. They asked me if I was satisfied. I was sure and hoped they were happy with me too. They mainly asked me to come to every women's evening.

When we broke up, the oldest woman asked if she could come with me in the car because I probably lived in her neighborhood. I asked how she knew that. She had seen me at supermarket once. When we arrived at her house, she asked if I would like another drink. I went inside and from a drink; it went to another drink and to a kiss to a French kiss. And soon, the blouses went out and we went upstairs where we undressed each other. Before her age (48), she still had a beautiful tight body with full overripe breasts and a lovely pussy to lick and play with. We went to bed and I was lucky that she was an experienced bi who let me experience all the pleasures of having sex with a woman.

Outside of the sex nights, we come together once a week and with a strap-on dildo in the shape of a dick, we make each other cum. We also agreed on her birthday and I asked her in advance which gift she would like to receive from me. She said I want something from you, but I will ask you on my birthday. On her birthday, we immediately went upstairs and pulled off each other's clothes. After a while, she asked what gift she wanted to get from me. I'd love to take you anal on his doggies. I was shocked because it didn't seem nice at all. My ex-boyfriend always wanted it and always refused it. But yes, she was always so sweet in bed for me that I decided to make an exception for her. Just kneel on the floor. Cup down, ass up. She smeared her fingers with oil and with one finger, she penetrated my butt hole. Then with a finger from her other hand and began to stretch my butt hole.

When she thought it was enough, she said now head up and with her 'dick,' she penetrated into my ass hole. That gave a lot of pain when she pushed on. Relax, you said she. She stepped back and pushed further inside. Always back a bit and then further inside until she could not continue. She then started riding me. I started to feel better and took over her role. I went back and forth with my ass over her 'dick.' You're the only one who can take me like that when she exhausted her 'dick' from my ass. Now I also wanted to take her like this and now it is true that from now on, we take each other in the pussy and then in the butt hole.

You understand that I no longer need sex with a man.

Chapter 3:

Last time I told you about my adventures with the sex club and my sexy girlfriend.

You will think what a young girl (23) does with a woman of 48 years. I saw that I had forgotten to mention her name. Her name is Morgan.

That relationship lasted a year and we both concluded that it was better than everyone went their own way.

I had started visiting the monthly women's night at the sex club again, although it became a bit monotonous because the same participants always came.

I also thought there was too little of the real thing and too much of making love and pampering each other with toys. The last time I was there, there were two newcomers — a couple of friends my age, Erica and Alexa both 24 years old. I found it that I ended up in a trio with one of those girls and finally found someone who wanted to go further than just making love and could take a beating. In the follow-up discussion with Erica and Alexa, we concluded that we were on a par. They lived together and invited me to meet each other on Saturday at their home.

Full of expectation, that Saturday at 7 a.m. They lived in a village in a single-family home. I rang the bell and was welcomed by the two girls. The three of us sat comfortably on the couch — me in the middle. We drank a few wines. They were very curious about my sex life so far and said they were both bi, but mostly lesbian.

Gradually we became more intimate and started kissing each other. As I kissed Erica, Alexa began to explore my body and I felt her hand slide over my breasts. Alexa took over the kissing and Erica started to untie the buttons on my blouse. She took off my blouse and loosened the closure of my bra. What wonderful breasts you have and started to suck and lick my nipples so that they became swollen and harder. In the meantime, they spread my legs and lifted my skirt so that my pants came out. Alexa put her hand on my pussy and stroked my pussy through the fabric. Erica slid her hand over my stomach and slipped into my pants. My pussy was wonderfully spoiled. I had to stand up and my skirt was taken off. If you turn around, we can admire your buttocks. They rolled my pants and spread my legs. They stroked the inside of my thighs and pussy. Erica put me back on the couch and started to lick my pussy. Erica spoiled my breasts.

After a few more wines, it was time to go upstairs. I was completely naked and Erica and Alexa were completely dressed.

We entered a room with a horizontal bar hanging in the middle that was attached to the ceiling with a rope.

All kinds of whips and carts stood on a table.

Two slats, one made of bamboo and one made of plastic that was so flexible that you could fold it almost double. You could swing with it.

Two carts, one with a dozen thin laces with a button every few centimeters.

The other had five slightly thicker laces with a steel bead every few centimeters.

Two thick whips, one of braided leather and the other of some kind of steel.

Two thin whips, one of leather and one with a thin metal wire.

I got a ring on my wrists and ankles. I had to grasp the rod at the two ends. The bands around my wrists were attached to the rod. A shelf was laid on the floor on which I had to stand. My legs were slightly spread and attached to rings on the shelf. My pussy was now clearly visible and accessible. The rod was pulled up until I was completely stretched and spread out.

Erica told what the intention was.

We will test you for your material knowledge. You see here for your eight attributes. We play for three rounds.

An attribute is used in each round. You get ten strokes — five from behind and five from the front. After each round, you have to say which attribute we used. If you are wrong, then we will start again until you have made the right choice. We have already played this game with five girls and one came after 40 strokes — the other between 50 and 70. You will, of course, be blindfolded. Unfortunately, we are forced to shut up because of the neighbors.

I was blindfolded and a ball in my mouth that was fastened with a strap around my head.

We are going to start shouting Erica.

Suddenly I felt a hard blow to my back. It must have been a quirt. I got my buttocks a second blow — two following on the inside of my thighs. The last one was the worst. She hit my butt like that through my legs to my pussy. I could scream in pain. I pulled in vain on the ties with which I was bound.

Then it was the front turn. Relentlessly I got a hard blow on my breasts. I winced as far as possible. The second and third blow came to my stomach. The last ones returned to my thighs. The blindfold was pushed and they showed me the two carts. With a big nod, I had to indicate which one was used. I thought the one with the five laces. I was wrong and they started again. The next round, I was treated with a bar. First two strokes on my buttocks and one on my stomach and two on the inside of my thighs. The worst was yet to come. I got hard blows right on my nipples and tried to scream but got no further than some murmuring. I got two strokes on the bottom of my breasts and one on my stomach. There was no doubt it was by no means the bamboo stick. It was true and I went to the final round.

It was a big whip now — two strokes on my back and two on my buttocks and one on my thighs.

On the front of my stomach and thighs, I gambled well; it was the leather whip.

I still don't understand how I went through everything. My whole body seemed to be on fire.

I was released and could barely stand on my legs. They supported me and brought me to a room next door. They were again sweet and wanted to help me take care of my skin. I just wanted one thing. Go home as quickly as possible. They helped me get dressed, which was very painful. They brought me to my car. With a lot of effort, I got behind the wheel. At the last minute, I received a certificate stating that I had participated and received 50 strokes. Those bad guys said I could get a second chance. I drove away quickly and stopped around the corner. I called Morgan and told me what happened.

She said she should come to her. When she arrived at her house, she was already waiting for me. She helped me out of the car and brought me inside. In her bedroom, she carefully undressed me. She gently took care of my skin — first, with ice cubes in the hottest spots on my body. Later she gently brushed me on with oil.

I stayed with her for two weeks and called my boss that I was sick.

After those weeks, I had already recovered nicely. We met again with great care.

The bad things were done now.

But I wasn't rid of those bad girls yet. One day I received mail. It was an invitation to attend the opening of the new establishment of a "theater" that those girls had started in an old farmhouse. Reference was also made to their new internet site.

Although I still hated those girls, I still went to the internet site. It said there were weekly shows. There were also photos on the site. To my horror, they saw that they had secretly taken photos when they beat me. Even up close so that my face and my entire naked body could be covered with red stripes. I was completely upset and fled to Morgan again.

Still there. For the outside world, I am her daughter from the marriage with her early deceased husband.

Nobody needs to know what we do at home and in bed.

FFM Threesome

Sonya and Maggie were drawn to each other from the beginning, and their secret relationship was full of heat. The only downside was Sonya's husband, Chris. When Chris sneaks home to spy on his wife, he does catch Sonya in bed with someone. What will he do when he discovers it is Maggie and not the pool boy?

I just love the way she feels curled up next to me. Her smooth skin sliding against mine, her soft curves pressed up against me. I know she's more than ten years younger than me, and I'm married and all that, but I just can't help but sink into whatever this is she and I share.

It started rather innocently, with her and her kids hanging out at our house for the pool. She is a single mom, and I felt bad for her. She moved in next door right after her divorce, and her daughters were about the age of mine so it just seemed the right thing to do.

One day her kids were with their dad and mine were at day camp, but she came over to swim anyway. She looked so amazing in her bikini, I could not take my eyes off her. I had fooled around with a couple of girlfriends in college, but nothing serious. But I really could not stop staring at her firm tits or smooth ass. I had no idea she was aware of my stares until she cornered me in the pool.

We had been drinking margaritas all afternoon (hey, don't judge, I was at home, and she only had to walk about twenty feet to her house). Her skin smelled like coconut oil, and her long dark hair clung wetly to her back.

"Sonya," she whispered as she backed me up against the edge of the pool.

"Maggie? What's going on?" I was a little startled, a little confused, and a little turned on by her nearness.

When she kissed me, I was surprised that I did not slide down into the water in surprise. But she was insistent and her hands on my waist held me in place while

I shivered from her touch. Well, the afternoon did not end there. We ended up naked in the pool and then making a mad dash for the house, giggling like schoolgirls. She and I spent that entire afternoon together, in the bedroom, in the shower, on the kitchen table. We were like horny teenagers all over the house.

We were all dressed and proper by the time my kids and husband got home, but that afternoon was just the beginning. Every chance we got, we were together. My husband thought it was nice that we were friends, and our kids seemed to get along so it all worked out very well.

Honestly, I do not know if I could ever give up men altogether, but Maggie was the closest thing I had ever had to a relationship with a woman and it seemed perfect. She was absolutely insatiable in her need for me, in all ways. For the most part, she behaved herself when the families were around, but she did like to tease me in subtle little ways.

Sometimes she would do something very simple, like run an ice cube over her neck so that her nipples stuck out under her thin tee shirt. Other times, she would sneak a grope under the table at dinner. And sometimes she would not do anything at all, and that drove me even crazier. I wanted her constantly, all the time, and in every way possible.

My husband traveled occasionally for work, and if I could convince a set of grandparents to take my kids for the weekend that her kids were with their dad, we had the whole weekend to ourselves. We spent the entire time naked, sometimes swimming, sometimes cuddled up under a blanket on the couch, and a good portion of the time in bed.

The affair went on for several months like that, she and I taking any opportunity to be together. It started to feel like we were getting emotionally involved too. I wanted to be with her even if we were not going to have sex. I liked going out to lunch and catching a movie and going shopping and all those things too.

My sex life with my husband started to change, and I think that was when he first started to notice something. He and I had always been very active sexually, even after we had kids. Since I do not work, I maintain my figure quite nicely and always have the energy for a roll in the hay. Since I started seeing Maggie, I was less and less interested in sex with him, though. I don't know if I just was not interested in sex with a guy, or not interested in sex with him in particular.

But he was getting suspicious so I talked to Maggie about it one afternoon as we cuddled on the couch.

"I don't know what to do. I'm just not interested in being with him, not since you, and I have been together."

"Oh Sonya," her sweet Southern accent drove me insane, "I don't want to mess up your marriage."

"It's not that, I'm an adult and make my own decisions. I just don't want what he has to offer."

Maggie giggled, "But you like what I have to offer?"

"Oh hell yes!"

I punctuated my affirmation by rolling her over and sliding my hand inside her little running shorts. She moaned softly, and the rest of the conversation was lost in my efforts to make her moan over and over again.

By the time Chris got home that night, she was already back home with a satisfied smile on her face. I did succumb to his advances that night, but it was less than enjoyable. The only reason I even gave in was because pleasing Maggie had left me horny as hell.

He gave me a strange look afterwards, but I just played sleepy and rolled away from him. I was going to have to talk to Maggie about calming things down. But the very idea of not seeing her anymore made me extremely sad. I already missed her soft tits and smooth ass, and she had only been gone a few hours.

****

The next day Maggie came back over around mid-day, after Chris went into work a little late. We made some lunch in the kitchen and then carried it outside to eat on the patio.

"Maggie," I said quietly.

"Yeah, I know. We need to back off. Right?"

I nodded sadly, "I think Chris might suspect something."

"But would he be upset since it's me and not another guy?"

"I have no idea what he would do."

We ate our sandwiches in silence, staring at the rippling blue water of the swimming pool. It was the pool boy's day to come clean, and if we were going to fool around, we needed to either get it done before he got there or wait until after he left. I looked down at her hand on the table, and covered her fingers with mine.

"I don't want to stop seeing you," I admitted softly.

"Me neither. I like that we're both friends and lovers. But I don't want to get you in trouble, or mess up your family."

"I know, me neither. And I appreciate you thinking of that."

She turned her hand around so that her fingers were entwined with mine. I looked into her pale blue eyes and sighed. I was helpless.

Maggie leaned over to kiss me, and her soft mouth chased away any thoughts I had of calling it quits. Within minutes, she was straddling my lap. I lightly tickled her tummy just inside her tee shirt and she wriggled for me, making her round tits bounce and jiggle.

I cupped one of them firmly, letting my thumb tease her stiff nipple. I loved making her moan, and I seemed to be pretty good at it.

"Inside," she whispered urgently as she rose up from my lap.

I grabbed her hand, and we dashed inside to the bedroom. Just as I closed the drapes, I heard the van pull up outside indicating that the pool boy had arrived. I looked over at Maggie and sighed. She shook her head and giggled, tugging her tee shirt back down in place.

After ordering her to stay put, I dashed downstairs to give him his check for the week. He grinned at me, stuck it in his pocket, and popped his earbuds back in.

When I got back upstairs, I tugged at Maggie's hand until she was standing in front of the draped window. I opened it slightly, and nestled my body behind hers. With a few inches of the window exposed, I started to tease Maggie.

My fingers tickled her inner thighs as I pressed my tits against her back. I was certain she could tell that I was not wearing a bra as she squirmed against me. She could see the young college boy skimming the pool surface with the big net, and she tried to close the drapes, but I caught her hands and moved them back to her sides.

Her little running shorts gave me easy access, and I slid my hand down her ass and between her legs. With one finger, I teased her pussy lightly and gently. She moaned as her head fell back against my shoulder.

With the pool boy just outside, I kept teasing her, knowing that he could look up at any time and possibly see us. My finger slipped inside her shorts and then inside her bikini bottom. She felt smooth and slippery under my touch. I teased all around her clit as my other hand snuck inside her tee shirt and rubbed her soft tits.

Pinching her nipple lightly, I finally grazed her clit with a feather touch. She gasped loudly and parted her legs further to silently encourage my fingers.

"Take me to bed," she whispered throatily.

She spun towards me, and we tumbled backwards onto the bed. Our arms and legs thrashed about as we removed our clothes and swimsuits. As soon as she was naked, I slid my body between her thighs and found my prize. She tasted like wildflower honey as I licked her, her fingers entangled in my hair.

Her moans filled the room as I teased her a little bit longer until her hips bucked towards me and her back arched in frustration.

"Please, Sonya, please," she begged.

I slid two fingers inside her wetness and caught her clit in my mouth. She groaned loudly and then screamed my name as she came for me. As soon as she crested the peak and caught her breath, she nimbly flipped me over and pressed her body against mine.

"I didn't get mine yesterday," she whispered, teasing me with just the tips of her fingers.

I groaned and wrapped my legs around her trim waist. She was sliding in and out of my wetness, teasing and tormenting me as I had done to her. When she finally buried two fingers inside, I moaned.

"Oh God yes, Maggie," I praised her talents.

It was only a few strokes before I was cumming for her, thrashing and digging my nails into her delicate skin. As we lay together afterwards, still entwined and smelling of each other, I brushed her unruly hair from her face as she licked my taste from her fingers.

"How can I give you up?" I whispered against her cheek.

Her hand lay flat against my pounding heart, "I don't know."

In that quiet moment, we both nearly came out of our skins when the bedroom door flew open and slammed into the wall.

"What the fuck is this?" the voice boomed.

Our heads snapped up to see Chris standing at the foot of the bed.

"I thought it was fucking pool boy! I knew this was his day, and I saw his van. But her?" his finger was leveled at Maggie.

I nodded, clutching Maggie closer against me.

"Chris…"

"What could you have to say to me?" his thick dark brows were knitted together.

"I never meant…"

"Never meant for me to find out?"

"Not this way. Please, don't be mad at her. It's not her fault." I was shielding the quivering woman in my arms.

His brows smoothed out, and his eyes took on a wicked gleam as he started to remove his clothing.

"I think you two owe me… It's my turn now…"

****

We watched him undress, since admittedly he does have a very nicely chiseled body. Maggie looked at me, and I squeezed her shoulder as I reached for Chris's hand. As much as I loved being with Maggie, I could not risk my marriage. If Chris was demanding an afternoon with both of us to save our marriage, then I was just hoping she would go along with me. As Chris slid into the bed next to me, Maggie reached over and pulled him between us. I smiled at her in a silent thank you.

He grinned down at her and slowly ran his hand up her bare hip. He turned towards my sexy friend and I curled up behind him. As he kissed her, I let my hands wander over his bare back. Maggie's arm snaked around his waist, and I entwined my fingers with hers. She squeezed my hand lightly and then withdrew it to cup my breast. I arched into her touch, and felt a surge of heat to my pussy as she moaned softly.

Chris finally broke away from her mouth to look back at me.

"How long has it been going on?" he wanted to know.

"A few months," I admitted, "but look at her, who could resist?"

I smiled down at my special friend.

When he kissed me roughly, I could taste a mixture of her lips and my pussy. It was intoxicating, and I let my tongue dance inside his mouth to taste more. When I finally pulled away, I followed Maggie's gaze to find her staring at my husband's generous cock. He was quite nicely endowed, and she almost looked intimidated. I giggled and pressed my tits up to his back so that we could see his cock surge thicker.

His hand dropped to encircle himself and stroke it lightly.

"Rather nice, hmm?" he winked at Maggie.

She nodded, letting just her fingertips tickle the head as he stroked. I reached around to knead his heavy balls. His cock swelled again as all three hands teased him.

"Oh damn," he moaned, slowing his strokes.

"What, baby?" I giggled, "Too much?"

"Um, maybe…" his cheeks flushed slightly, not used to all of the stimulation.

"Well, what have you imagined in a threesome?" I was curious since all straight men fantasize about it.

"I'm, um, not sure."

He had stopped stroking and was just holding himself as Maggie, and I teased him.

"Four hands? Two mouths?"

His cock bobbed at my suggestions.

I clamored off the bed, leaving Chris and Maggie alone for just a moment. When I returned, I was carrying the fuzzy handcuffs that he had given me years ago as a gag gift.

"What if we just have our way with you?" I swung the cuffs in front of his face.

His eyes lit up hungrily, "I could do that."

Maggie and I rolled him onto his back and cuffed his wrists to the headboard. His cock bobbed and surged as we knelt over him.

Maggie leaned over to me in a loud whisper, "Do we just tease him and then please each other?"

I laughed as Chris pulled on the handcuffs and his cock twitched.

"It's a good start," I winked at her.

We both knelt between his spread thighs, his thick cock stretching up to his lower abs. She gently pushed on his shins and thighs until he was in a rather awkward position, as though he was about to give birth. She knelt to one side, and I stayed in between his thighs. When my mouth wrapped around his balls and hers engulfed his cock, I thought he was going to rip the bed apart.

"Oh fuck, fuck, fuck," he groaned as our tongues danced wetly over the most sensitive parts of him.

Slowly we sucked and licked him until he was barely able to breathe. We hovered him right at the edge, and kept him perched there with slow wet teasing. Surrounding him with wet heat was going to push him over, so we backed off and just licked and tickled him. He twisted against the cuffs, trying to shove his cock into one of the mouths that tormented him.

"Oh God, please, please," he kept pleading, bucking his hips towards our mouths.

When I thought we could no longer hold him at the edge, I gently pulled her face from my husband's cock and kissed her deeply. On our knees over his body, we kissed, our tongues entwined between our lips. My hands roamed over her smooth skin, tightly cupping her ass as her fingers pinched my nipples.

Chris bucked on the bed, desperate for his turn. We pretended to ignore him as my hand slipped between her thighs. I broke off kissing her to describe her to Chris.

"Oh Chris, she's so slippery and wet and tight. I can barely slide two fingers inside that hot silk."

His cock bobbed between us, twitching and dripping.

"Are you interested in fucking my sweet Maggie?" I asked him softly.

"Oh fuck, yeah," his eyes were roaming her full breasts and slender waist.

I kept sliding two fingers in and out of her pussy, making sure my thumb grazed against her swollen clit.

"Do you want to see me make her cum?"

"Oh God, oh God," he was twisting in his handcuffs.

With one hand teasing his full balls, I plunged the other into her pussy hard and fast until she was quaking and moaning my name. As she eased down, I slowly withdrew my hand and licked one finger clean.

"God, you taste so good, my sweet Maggie," I looked at Chris as I said it.

"Touch my cock," he was begging.

Very few men can tolerate having their balls teased without something touching their cock. I can't even imagine how torturous it was when he had just finished watching me finger my girlfriend. I ignored his request and kept kneading the heavy sac.

Maggie leaned to me and whispered, "Can I suck him?"

"Already?" I giggled.

"Yeah, then I want to taste you and get him all hard again so he can fuck me."

I nodded, "Have at it."

She fell between his thighs and sunk her mouth down his shaft as far as it would go. His hips bucked upwards, and I knew this was going to be quick. I held her hair back so that he could watch her cheeks pull in as she sucked hard. Chris's eyes were rolled back in his head when I pressed my thumb up to that spot just between his sac and his asshole.

I leaned up to his ear and whispered to him, "Her tongue is amazing, isn't it? I love it on my clit, you know."

He grunted loudly as his balls tightened up against his body and she pulled back off his cock. With our combined four hands, we stroked him fast and hard until he erupted on her tits.

"Fuuuuuuuck," he groaned loudly, straining at his bonds as jet after jet splashed on her soft mounds.

Just as he was easing back to reality, Maggie crawled up next to him. With her fingers lightly tickling his twitching abs, she whispered in his ear.

"Hey big fella, I want you to watch me eat your sexy wife's beautiful pussy. Then I hope your cock is good and ready to fuck me."

I felt my own juices dripping down my thighs as I heard her filthy words to my husband. His extended cock twitched at the images she gave him.

I knelt on the bed next to his hips, facing him. Maggie stretched out along his legs so that her face was nestled between my parted thighs. Chris's eyes widened as he watched her slowly run her tongue up my slippery slit.

"Oh she gets so wet for me," Maggie grinned up at me with a glossy smile.

I felt another surge of moisture as I looked down at her. When her tongue teased just inside my pussy, I felt my thighs tremble. In and out like a tiny soft cock, she teased me. I closed my eyes as I moaned, bracing myself on Chris's bent knee. She caught my clit between her lips and tugged lightly, letting the tip of her tongue flicker over the taut surface.

"Oh, yes, like that, yes," I breathed.

Faster and harder, her tongue drew tiny circles until I screamed and dug my nails into Chris's exposed thigh.

"Oh fuck," he and I groaned together.

She slid out from underneath me with a grin. It was all I could do to collapse forward onto my husband's chest.

He raised his head as far as it would go and whispered to me, "I have the hottest wife ever."

I stroked my hand down his flat stomach until I reached the head of his reawakened cock.

"It appears he is ready for you," I grinned at Maggie.

She quickly straddled him and lowered her tight little pussy onto his thickness.

"Oh sweet fuck," he moaned, surging his hips upwards.

I stretched out next to him to watch. Despite my interest in Maggie lately, he was pretty good in bed. I loved being able to watch both of them please each other. Her tits were bouncing deliciously, and he was thrusting madly up inside her.

I reached up and unfastened the cuffs to release his hands. They instantly fell to squeeze her breasts and then to hold her steady while he pounded her. I knelt over his torso and kissed her, tasting myself on her lips and tongue.

Her head fell away from me as she moaned, "Oh fuck, oh shit, oh Sonya, Chris, oh my God."

I reached between their bodies and pressed my finger to her clit, rubbing the tight tiny circles I knew would send her over the edge. And it did. She bucked and screamed and clawed at Chris and I. Eventually she fell forward onto his chest, and I stroked her hair softly.

"Now it's your turn," Chris's gaze was wicked and hungry and intense.

We gently rolled Maggie to the side, and she curled up into his warm body. I crawled on top of him, holding his cock steady as I slid my pussy around him. He was slick with her juices and the thought sent me spiraling instantly into my climax. His fingers dug into my hips as he thrust his full length inside me.

"Cum for me, Sonya," he ordered.

I caught my breath and stared down at him intently.

"Now fuck me," I demanded.

We scrambled into our favorite position, doggie-style, slightly altered so that Maggie was underneath my kneeling body.

She kissed and stroked my body as he tore into my pussy with that steel cock of his. She pinched my nipples and stroked my clit as his cock stretched me with each thrust. I stared into her eyes, and as I surged into my next climax, she held me tightly and kissed me. It felt as though I was coming with both of them at the same time.

Chris dug his nails into my hips and thrust one more time, and I felt the surge of his climax as the jets washed through my pussy. We collapsed simultaneously, each falling to one side of Maggie. She rolled towards me and wrapped her arms around me, and Chris curled up behind her.

****

We must have dozed off because it was several hours later when we woke up, still tangled up with each other. Maggie and I woke first, and snuck off the bed as quietly as we could.

Once we were dressed and downstairs, she kissed me firmly.

"Oh Sonya, I'm so glad he did not get too mad," she whispered against my neck.

"Me too, Maggie. I'm not ready to give up either one of you."

She nuzzled my throat, and I squirmed under her warm breath.

Eventually, Chris woke up as well and joined us downstairs.

"Well, ladies, that was quite the adventure."

We both nodded, shuffling our flip flops since we did not really know where he was headed.

"And I think I'm okay with this," he gestured to the two of us.

"But," he continued, "I do want to be a part of it sometimes."

Maggie looked at me with questions in her eyes. I guess the decision was up to me, whether I wanted to share my girlfriend and my husband with each other.

I kissed her sweetly and then walked over to kiss him too.

"I can't lose either one of you, and you seem to like each other as well. I think this could work out."

They both grabbed me in an awkward three-way hug.

Eventually, my kids came barreling through the front door from day camp, and hers returned from their time with their dad. Both families spent the rest of the weekend in the pool and on the back porch together, grilling hamburgers and splashing each other with the cool water in the pool. Now that the secret was out, it did not seem awkward anymore. It just seemed like very good friends hanging out.

Maggie and I were still very careful to hide our closeness from all of the kids. That would just bring up questions none of us were ready to answer.

But Maggie and I still saw each other as often as we could manage, and Chris would join us when the opportunity presented itself.

About a year after that first afternoon, we all decided to get a bigger house together. The financial help would benefit both families, and with the combined household income we could afford assistance with the pool, the house, and the small yard. All of the kids got along great, and none of them seemed the wiser that it was possibly an odd arrangement.

The only rule I had put into place was that they were not allowed to sleep together without me. For some reason, in my head, that seemed more like cheating than anything else. Chris agreed surprisingly easily, and I was grateful. I guess maybe he was just glad it was not the pool boy.

I did sometimes worry that Maggie was so caught up in Chris and I that she would not seek out a relationship of her own.

I brought it up over margaritas one evening after the kids were all in bed.

"Oh Sonya, you are sweet to worry. But truthfully, I'd prefer to find a guy who could be a part of this. I don't know exactly what this is, but I love you both. I would not want a relationship of my own that damaged the three of us."

I kissed her lightly on the nose and tucked her hair behind her ear.

"We love you too," I murmured.

"So how do I find a guy who can make our fabulous threesome a foursome?"

I laughed, "Maybe a golf course?"

A Desirable Night

I spent a few days completely immersed in work, stopping every so often just to look at the plaque on my desk that said, "Paige Webster - Lawyer". So, when Brett invited me to dinner at Parry. Parry was the most luxe and one of the most talked-about restaurants in the city. I fell from the clouds, I never thought he would take me to such an exquisite place. It was an odd gesture for Brett as he liked to maintain a very low profile, avoiding most gala evenings and other social events.

He didn't give me time or a way to change, so I found myself at dinner, in one of the most fashionable restaurants in the city, in the same dress I had worn all day at work. The dinner was nothing short of perfect, and not only for the excellent courses. Brett did not say a single word that could relate to work, pulling out his ironic and almost unconventional personality. I also discovered, and to my great surprise, that he knew all the gossip of the upper-middle class, with a particular fondness for stories of tawdry affairs.

His stories only stopped when he went to the bathroom, and in those moments, I thought of how little I knew him since he was able to amaze me in that way.

"Shall we go to yours," He asked after returning from the restroom, taking me completely by surprise.

"Yes," I replied as I stood up a little upset over his proposal.

We took the short drive in an almost awkward silence, but once in my apartment, Brett became a real man, as perhaps he had never been.

"Give me your panties," He said as if it were an order while taking off his jacket and tie.

I raised my skirt to take off my thong, and then I leaned forward slightly, almost putting my ass in his face. He reached out and gently rubbed my vagina, running his fingers through the gap.

"My God, how beautiful you are," he said, groping my bottom.

"Brett," I Started.

"Shh, tonight you will be mine, and not as you usually are," he told me, wetting a finger that I immediately found against the hole of my ass. "Tonight, I want to use you as my personal whore, and you will never tell me no."

With that, I folded, even more, opening my legs after removing the skirt which was now only a hindrance. He, however, was as if he were stuck, in fact, he could not be as dominant as he wanted to be in words. In fact, not only did he not sodomize me in any way despite having placed his finger on my anus, but he started kissing my ass with love.

"What the fuck are you doing," I told him with contempt, "have you ever seen a whore to kiss her ass? So, now put that finger in me and take out your pecker or you can go home and jerk yourself off instead."

I had stricken Brett's pride, so he spit upon my ass and let his finger slide inside me.

"Be like that, I like you," I told him, taking off my blouse and bra before I got down on the couch. "Now take your dick out so I can suck you until you feel it in your soul."

Brett looked like a cross between a robot and a child in a store toy. Not only did he follow all my instructions, but he was almost incredulous at being able to do it, not realizing that I was actually leading the game, knowing full well that he was certainly not a dominant. In fact, after a short blowjob and an equally quick fingering of my ass, he sat down not knowing what to do.

So, he settled me on top of him, and after grabbing his cock with one hand, I impaled myself by giving him my back to stick his shaft up my ass.

"I want your pussy," he said to me in amazement as I was riding him.

"Don't whores do it like this, but tonight I am your bitch," I replied, taking his hand to bring it on my wetness. "Or maybe, that's not what you want, don't you want to take me as the others did before you."

"You're right, you're just a bitch that has to be treated as such. Put yourself on all fours on the ground which is the only thing you know how to do."

I got up to get on all fours on the ground, and to make him even more excited, with one hand I opened the little hole while with the other I started masturbating with passion.

"What are you waiting for with your cock in your hand! Put it in my ass and make me enjoy it!"

"Here you are served, queen of whores."

He put the tip against my back opening, then grabbed me firmly by the sides, before pushing himself in with all the rage he had in his body.

"Please make me enjoy, make me your bitch," I yelled in a mixture of pain and pleasure that I found irresistible.

Contrary to what I had thought, Brett inculcated me for a long time, also because sometimes he took out his cock to replace it with two or three fingers, which dilated me more. By now it had almost become a battle with him trying to delay his orgasm as much as possible, and I urged him to possess me as a true dominant male. At one point; however, it seemed clear to both of us that he just couldn't come, so I made him sit on the couch allow him to catch his breath.

As soon as he breathed, he returned to regular, I took his cock in my hand and started licking his balls, while I masturbated him very calmly. When I saw him moan louder, I abandoned his testicles to lick his penis, but never took it completely in my mouth, covering it only with saliva.

"Now I'll let you enjoy it," I told him, sitting down on him, as I had done before, but this time using my vagina, which received his penis without offering any resistance.

I was thankful that he had been brutal, so now I was sweet, riding him with almost exasperating slowness, but that allowed us to kiss relentlessly, while our hands searched each other's' body. In the end, he came inside me and seemed almost ashamed of it, but a caress of mine was enough to make him smile again.

Brett dressed again without saying a word, only to break the silence with a question that left me astounded.

"How did you know about my foot fetish?"

Not knowing what to answer, I decided to tell him the truth, from the chance encounter with Shannon. I told him everything about that encounter and the day after. Brett listened intently without ever interrupting me, then dressed and as if it were nothing asked me to meet with him the next day at the office.

I could not get to sleep thinking all the time if I had done well to tell him the truth, even though I could not go back on it now. At half-past two, the phone rang to give me the news that it would change my life.

"Brett had a fatal accident," were Amelia's few words to me. They threw me into despair, leaving me only the strength to dress to go to the hospital where I found almost all the lawyers from the office.

"Now that Brett is gone there will be a war of power without end." Finley Allen told me after taking me aside. "You should never take a position, and see that you become almost invisible or you'll be the first to go. If Amelia takes control of the law firm for you there will be room, otherwise, you should probably look for a new job."

"Why?"

"If Porsei wins, he will not want anyone around to obscure him, he just wants power and definitely doesn't want anyone around who might take that from him. Amelia, on the other hand, doesn't care about that, for her only the divorce money counts, and with them, she can also cover some losses."

"But now who will follow Sophia Hayes' case against Steele?"

Finley said a blasphemy that almost opened a crack on the ceiling of the hospital, but I had just reminded him that keeping a low profile was almost impossible. This was because Brett had taken the case of a young girl, who had been nearly enslaved by a rich and powerful family of entrepreneurs. She had found the courage to denounce her captors, but would not even be defended by Amber's father, who was currently the best lawyer in the city.

Finley consulted quickly with Amelia and then returned to me.

"The case is yours, so if you lose it will not be great damage to your image. The Steele family is defended by Simmons and you are on your first case without Brett, so it's a well-calculated risk."

"But I want to win!"

"I know and I hope you succeed, mainly because you don't know how much I hate Simmons. But you will take care of this after the funeral, now it is only time to cry for a friend more so than a colleague."

I stayed a couple of hours close to what I hoped would become my new protector, without knowing what to do except talk about as little as possible and try to hide the pain I had inside. Not even the arrival of Jasmine was of any comfort to me, deciding at the end to go home to prepare both for the funeral, and for my new case, the first one I faced without having Brett near me.

Hunting in the Bar

I was standing at the bar that I used to frequent when I spied on a group of young people. They were older than college girls. I assumed it was one of the 'Girls Night Out' events. All the girls were attractive, but as I watched, there were only three of them who accepted the men's dances and drinks. The fourth was the most attractive: tall, slim, long black hair, pointed nose, and good tits and butt. No part of it was that unique, but the parts fit well together.

After an hour of repeated rejection on her part, the one girl got up. I thought maybe she was leaving, but she moved to a table that had never been occupied before. She was looking really sad. Maybe her move was intended to get away by herself, but it didn't work. Instead, the men seemed to think that they could separate one from the herd, and the predators moved in. I haven't seen them in the bar before. The first two pursuers were shot away by the girl. The third one was more persistent. Obnoxiously. Her "No" was getting louder and I could see her face getting angry and angry.

I moved before I realized that I had made a decision to intervene. "Hi, sweetheart, I 'm sorry I 'm late." I kissed her quickly on her mouth, hoping she wouldn't be shocked. Before he could note her facial expression, I turned to the man and said, "I appreciate you holding my girl company. Thank you, my name is Rick." I put out my hand to shake. He's been in shock.

Luckily, the girl caught up with me and cooperated. "Rick, it's about time that you showed up. I was almost ready to leave."

The guy chimed in, "Yeah, it's crap that you've left such a pretty girl alone for so long. You don't have to worry about her very much."

"You 're completely right. I was supposed to learn about the five-car-pile on the I-24 in advance. I had to waste my time to use my CPR / First Aid expertise on two of the victims before the EMTs arrived. I think I'm going to have to make sure I speak to my therapist more frequently." The discussion with the prick soon turned out to be an adversarial.

I saw a group of guys at the bar that I had seen and spoken to before. I gave them a drink, and they returned the gesture. I said to the girl, "You don't need to worry dear, my friends said they'd keep an eye out before I got here." The guy looked at the men at the bar, lowered his level of animosity, and walked away.

The girl turned to me. "Thanks for the rescue. I don't think the kiss was too much to pay for your knight on the shining armour routine."

"Well, I thought it would be more believable if we kissed. Besides, I wanted to kiss you, and that might be my only chance ever. If you're sweet, I could let you kiss me back." She sat silently, but a smile took over her face before I went on.

"Girlfriend, I think that's the part where we introduce each other, find out how many things we have in common, and then make plans for a real date."

"Well, my name is Clarice and why does it seem like we are in a play where you have the script, but I don't?"

"D.W., which stands for Dwayne Warren, and is named 'Improv.'" she laughed.

"Damn you, D.W., I came here tonight to have a miserable time, wallowing in my self-pity. You've gone now and ruined it all, making me laugh."

"I 'd be happy to wallow with you if that's what you'd want. For the record, my reason for self-pity is that my fiancée left me two weeks before we got married. It seems like my best man was the best man."

"Ouch. That's horrible, but I might be able to top it off. I caught my boyfriend cheating on my mother!"

We both started to laugh. I said, "We seem to be a perfect couple. I just don't know what we're perfect for, except someone else's being screwed."

"Rick, because of our obvious misfortune, we 'd probably mess each other up. One of us would try to screw the clockwise and the other the clockwise." We laughed again.

I was taking a shot. "There's one way we can find out about that."

"Since it would be crazy, completely against my normal way of doing things, and consistent with what's happened in the last few minutes, let's do it. I need a good fucking revenge, and you seem to need one, too. Do you have a car with a big back seat?"

"You 're not going to be more relaxed in a bed?"

"I don't want to wait that long. I might lose my nerve.

We went out to the car, got in my back seat, and got screwed. I can't believe I've been as long as I've been. She started crying after we finished. I asked, "What's wrong with that? Was I that bad?"

"No, you were all right. I just can't believe that I gave myself to a perfect stranger."

"At least you think I was perfect," he said to me, but he was smiling.

"So, D.W., am I just another thing?"

"I don't know what you are except a great lover. It seems a little backward, but I'd like to know more about you before we make love again."

"You think we're going to have sex again, are you?"

"I 'm sure I hope so, don't you?"

"I don't know what to think about right now. Why don't you give me your phone number? I'm not going to give you mine, so I can determine how this relationship is going."

"All right." I wrote down my phone number. She straightened herself up and went inside with her parents. I sat down for a while and wondered what had just happened. In a couple of minutes, I saw her go out and drive away with two other girls.

She eventually called after three days. She said, "Okay, here's the deal. You 're going to take me out to a nice restaurant, one that you think will impress me, and then we're going to go to a coffee shop and chat."

"And then, then?"

"I'm going to decide after we talk."

"Oh goodie, I've got an audition."

"There's only one part available so you're better off not messing up."

I brought her to the grungiest little Chinese restaurant, which I was sure she had never heard of before. "Oh, D.W., your chances of getting the part just got slimmer. If the food isn't decent, you 're paying for a cab to take me home."

The family who owned the restaurant loved me. I spoke a little Mandarin they loved to hear me try and mess up terribly. They valued the effort. We didn't have to make an order. They've brought seven courses to our table. After course four, Clarice was full, but we didn't want to be impolite. After only charging $20 for both of us, we waddled out.

"So, some coffee shop or some taxi?"

"Should we go to a coffee shop? I need to start losing some calories after that meal," she said. "She saw the mischievous look in my eyes. "And don't you dare suggest that we can burn calories in another way, you pervert."

"Hey, don't blame me. Dirty minds think the same thing." She hooked her arm in mine all the way to the coffee shop.

Until the recent breakups, we each shared our life story. I can't really say that we have opposites, but we were definitely different. I think what we had most in common was our sense of humour. That night, we laughed a lot.

It was the closing time before we knew it. She looked very sad. I asked, "Should we call it a night?" I knew what she was going to say.

"It's the night."

"That's way too corny."

"I 'm sorry."

I took her home and we kissed her for a while. We both sighed, and she walked in. I've been in love.

We've been dating for six months and the last three were exclusive. I called with the ring in my pocket and asked if I should come over one night. I figured I was able to answer the issue. I stopped by the florist and walked to her house. She was opening the door. Her lipstick was smudged, and some of her blouse buttons were undone. There was a strong smell of alcohol. Standing in the middle of the room was a man I 'd never seen before. I figured he had something to do with the smudged lipstick.

Before she could say something, I shouted, "Who is that?"

She slurred, "That's my boyfriend, I mean my ex-boyfriend. Thank you for the flowers. Here let me put them in water." She fumbled the handoff and the roses fell to the floor. As she picked up the flowers, she said, "You can give me a hand. I'm a little bit tricky." She looked to see me shut the door on my way out. I know a man wasn't supposed to run away, but I didn't want her to see me crying. I made it to the parking lot until she was on the balcony of the apartment building, pleading for me to stop. I didn't do it.

My mobile phone was ringing. I didn't want her to hear me sobbing at all. I was so angry, I did a dumb thing, and I threw my cell phone out of the window. The next day, I went to replace my phone and decided to change my phone number. I informed my receptionist at work that I can no longer take calls from Clarice. She tried to call a couple of times and asked my secretary to tell me, 'It wasn't what it looked like.' Geez, she couldn't think of something more original.

I went to a bar other than the one where Clarice and I met. I was searching for a ranking. My desperation was evident when I was shot down, even by ugly, fat girls. I 'd hate to hear what they were saying about me. I thought it was easier to drink at home and have my pity party on my own.

I was told one day at my office that I had a call from Darren Jones. The name was not ringing a bell. "How can I help you, Mr. Jones?"

"I'm trying to help you right now. I'm Clarice's ex-boyfriend. She asked me to call and tell you what really happened that night when you came by. It wasn't what you thought."

I've been ready to hang up. I wondered if there was a Thesaurus included in the Cheater 's Handbook. I hesitated, and I let him go on.

"I had dropped by unannounced to apologise to Clarice and to assure her that my romancing her mother was not an attempt to provoke her. I told her that I really cared for her mother and wanted to continue to see her. I tell you, man, that her mother is even better than Clarice. Anyway, she was surprised that I was there, but she was interested in what I had to say about me and her mother.

Fuck! Shit! Just as I began to move on with my life. I started dialling her number a few times and gave it up. I just didn't want to open that worm can again. A few days passed by, and there was a knock on the door. I had the premonition that this was Clarice. It was her friend Allison, instead. She barked past me in a huff.

She turned to me and said, "This is from Clarice." She went on to kiss me passionately. As I pulled back in shock, she went on to say, "This is from me."

Allison was kicking me around the chest. I realised I was going to lose my hearing in the ear nearest to her blow. I've been speechless.

"You son of a bitch. Clarice is a mess. She hasn't gone back to work since the day you left. She's already lost ten pounds since she didn't eat. If she doesn't go back to work soon, she's going to lose her job, and that's all your fault."

"My fault? She was the one who had been with her boyfriend when she realised I was coming over. If she chose him over me, there was no question."

"And you didn't give her a chance to explain it. Didn't you call Darren?"

"Yes , yes."

"Oh, why didn't you call her?"

"I didn't believe it."

"Then it's a good thing that you're gone. I just hope I can keep her from hurting herself too much. Maybe now she can find someone who cares enough to talk about problems and not just run away," she said.

Later that night, I sucked up my ego and called Clarice. I apologised to her and she to me for weeping on both sides. We agreed to start by agreeing to speak to her if she ever did anything to make me angry. She vowed to be more cautious with the rest of the men. Three months later, I suggested it, and she accepted it.

The first few years of our marriage life were great, even though Clarice was still going overboard to convince me of her loyalty. I didn't mind spoiling a little. Both of us stepped up in our jobs and, thus, in our salaries. It was getting close to the time to think about having babies.

Clarice had gotten close to a few of the women she had worked with. We started having a Girls Night Out once a week. I was a little concerned, but I was asked to come and check on her a couple of times. She's always watched how much she's been drinking, and never seemed to get out of hand. I just stopped moving.

There was a bachelorette party for one of the women one night. Clarice came home late, sweaty on the trot. She woke me up and nearly raped me. No foreplay, straight to the fuck. She was so hot, I just fell in. It's been fast and furious. As both of us were climaxing, she went to sleep easily. I swept up the mess and put down a dry towel where the wet spot was.

The next day, I asked what caused her attack last night, and she said, "The male strippers got me all horny for you."

"Have you been acting yourself?"

"How could I not keep an eye on me with your watchdog Geneva? I didn't do anything she didn't do." Geneva was one of Clarice 's friends that I trusted. She is our Associate Pastor 's wife. I've always teased her that she was the guardian of Clarice when they left. I admit that I still felt a little uneasy.

Around two weeks later, there was another Girls Night Out, and I was welcomed again. I replied ambiguously that I might be coming. When it was time to go, I pretended to be part of a project at my office. Geneva picked her up, and both of them waved good-bye to me. I went and washed up an hour later. It was confidence, but it was time to check.

The place was crowded, but I finally found the crew. As I approached, my smile turned upside down really easily. Clarice was sitting in Darren 's lap, kissing him. Allison saw me as I stood staring at him and told Clarice. Darren dumped her on the floor of the building. I used to spin tires until I heard either Allison or Clarice call after me.

On the way home, I didn't obey speed limits. I packed a bag quickly, put my house key and the wedding ring on the dining table, and headed for a no-name motel. This time, I kept my phone, but I turned it off. I just had two drinks before I tried to go to sleep. It didn't take me too long to know what I was going to do on Monday.

I looked at my phone Monday morning and, as planned, there were multiple calls from Clarice, one from Allison, and one from Clarice 's mother. I deleted all of them. I called a friend who recently got divorced and asked for a divorce solicitor. At 2:00 a.m. I began sharing my tale of woe and I got the ball rolling on an expedited divorce with the 50/50 norm split. I was hoping she wasn't going to compete.

In contrast to the last time, I called her to give her a chance to explain. I was hoping she wouldn't say, 'It wasn't exactly what it looked like.'

"Hi, Clarice. I 'm giving you a chance to explain, so you're not going to complain that I haven't given you a chance to tell me a good story."

"Thank you for that, Rick. It was another case of bad timing. It wasn't what it looked like." I almost hung up after hearing that.

"We had our normal Girls Night Out when Mother and Darren came in. They were celebrating their engagement. Mom began buying drinks and I got more buzzed than usual. Just before you came in, I mocked Darren about being my step-father instead of my husband. He asked, 'Why don't you sit on your daddy's lap and congratulate me?' It seemed totally innocent, and we were intimate.

"Now, you can see that it was really nothing to get upset about. Maybe I shouldn't have sat in Darren 's lap and maybe I shouldn't have kissed him, but damn it, Rick. We were going to be married at one time. Now he's going to be part of my family. Cut me a little slack. Come home and let's work on building trust in our marriage."

"So, I'm supposed to believe that crap story?"

"It's not a story. It's the truth. Ask Allison. Ask my mother."

"If I don't believe you, the one person in the world I want to trust, then how am I going to believe the two people who want to help you the most? The ones that are more likely to lie and make you look good. No, I've given you a second chance. That's all the chances I can afford to give." I hung up.

There were no phone calls from her this time. I was so happy. I called her to work on Wednesday morning and asked if she had come to work that day. I told my lawyer once that was verified. Around 11:00, Clarice was greeted around a loud-speaking official who declared, 'You have been greeted with a DIVORCE PETITION CITING ADULTERY as a CAUSE.' It cost a little more, but he reported her response and it of her co-workers. Everything was worth everything.

I got a call from her around 11:15, as planned. She wasn't happy to say the least. "Actually, you had me served in my office for the greatest embarrassment. And what's this adultery crap? I didn't commit adultery, and you still can't file adultery as a cause in this state."

"Ooops, my bad."

"You obviously don't want to have children with me if you're going all the gangbusters for a minor mistake on my part. It's better to move on so that I can find a man who acts like a human and you can find a 'perfect' woman who doesn't make mistakes. That's what I thought love was—forgive the mistakes of the person you love.

"I 'm going to have a lawyer look at the complaint and have him come back with you. I hope we should decide on a split close to what you have suggested so that we can get it done as quickly as possible.

"Thank you. Come and see you at the meeting.

We ended up selling the house and splitting up the meager equities. Neither of us could afford mortgages, insurance and utilities on our own incomes. I had to consent to more rent than I had expected. Both of us would have to be frugal before we found a partner or a spouse to help share expenses and provide more income. Finding someone else was just the last thing on my mind. I worried about Clarice and Darren until I got an invitation to the marriage of Clarice's mother and Darren. The florist however, refused to place poison ivy in the flowers, so I wound up not sending anything.

I spent the next few months getting my new apartment furnished to suit my needs. It looked like a typical bachelor pad, a sparsely furnished bachelor pad. I received a note from one of the people I worked with. "Rick, I was sorry to hear about your divorce. As you probably know, a few months ago, I suffered the same thing. If you ever want to compare notes, I like Italian food. Marci.' Marci was just a few years older than me, a fine-looking woman. All of her curves were in the right places, although she generally dressed conservatively. I asked her to go out on a date. She accepted it.

I was in a good mood looking in the mirror as I was planning for my date. This will be my first official move forward. My phone was ringing. Would that be a Murphy call?

"Rick, we've got to talk."

"Clarice, I thought we were doing that at the divorce settlement. You 're asking for more money, because if you ...

"Shut up! It's serious." I heard a deep sigh. "I'm pregnant with you."

It was time for me to take a deep breath. "Congratulations to you and to Darren. What does your mother think of this?"

"Asshole! I've never had sex with Darren. She's your child. I'm over two months late."

"This is the thing that trusts again. Sorry, but I have trouble believing that I am the father."

"Well, you better believe it. Of course, I expect you to get the DNA test completed unless, of course, you don't trust the tests either."

"You 're right about that. Please tell me when the tests are done so that I can give my blood for a match, OR NOT. Is there anything else now? I have a date that I'm getting ready for."

"I hope the bitch is rich because you're going to get socked with a lot of child support. I have twins."

I have a snap picture of my bank statement in my head. Child support for two children. I'm going to have to start delivering pizza at night. "I don't know what to say about that."

"I've been thinking about this a lot for the last couple of days. I've got a proposal for you. You 're going to hate it, I 'm sure, but you might like the alternative even less. I don't want this baby alone. Allison and mother can help, but I want my husband, the baby's father, to be here for me. I'm proposing that you move in with me and your mother to save your home costs. As you remember, my mother has a big house.

"What's with the divorce?"

"I checked with my lawyer. If we both agree, we can have a six-month delay in the final decree. By then, you'll know the children are yours, and you can make a decision to run away again or not."

"I haven't run away. I have fled." I paused. "Let me think about it and come back to you."

"In the interest of full disclosure, I need to continue on your health insurance. I can't get new health coverage if I'm pregnant at the time of application."

"It actually makes me feel better. I was afraid that you might try to convince me that you wanted my back because you loved me."

"Bastard!"

"Bitch!"

Guess how that night my date with Marci went. "Oh, my goodness, Rick. What happened? You look like your dog is gone."

"Close. It was the rabbit of Clarice."

"Huh? Oh, no. Is she pregnant?"

"Oh, yeah."

"Is that yours?"

"Thank you for not automatically thinking that it was. The truth is, I don't know. It depends on how unfaithful she was right before I left. Technically, it's possible."

"What are you going to do now?"

"It's between suicide and running away right now. Of course, I could run away and commit suicide."

"Rick, I know you better than that. You 're not the man I think you are if you did one of those things. When will you know for sure?"

"Around five more months. Knowing Clarice, she's not going to agree to DNA testing before they're born. Too dangerous to the fetus."

"We are?"

"Actually, she has twins."

"My goodness, could things get more complicated?"

"Please don't tempt Murphy to make my life worse. Can we enjoy dinner and talk about something other than my misery?"

"We should do it."

We were trying. We've failed. In the house, there was a herd of elephants. After dinner, I took her home. I kissed her softly on her lips. I gave up on being able to go any further with her a long time ago.

"Rick, I'm going to pray for you. I hope you understand that I can't get involved with you until your problem is resolved. If the twins aren't yours and you get divorced, please contact me first. I really think we 're going to make a good couple."

My decision was made for me by the transmission of my car. $2,000 to fix it. I didn't have to spare $2,000. I called Clarice and agreed to move in and consolidate my living quarters. I caught a break (Yeah for the home team) and didn't have to pay for violating my contract. My landlady was a softie, and she almost cried when I told her about the condition I was in. Yeah, most of my tears were actual.

At first, I was awkward to re-establish a household routine with a woman I had lived with before she was pregnant. Now, she was a hormonal mess. Cravings, grumpy, weepy, horny and so on. I haven't been able to deny her in bed. It was hard to say, "Please stop sucking my cock, dear though it feels very good." I began to have more oral and anal sex with her when we couldn't have normal sex. I agreed that if by any miracle / disaster we ended up remaining together, anal and oral would be on the main menu. Although we did have sex, we did not exchange any word of love. There were plenty of: "Oh my gods," "Wow, that really felt greats," and "That was the best ever."

The day has finally arrived. Double voltage was present in the air: safe transmission and parentage. As usual, the twins arrived early and were a little underweight. Second, I saw the little girl coming out. She was looking a lot like Clarice. When the boy came out, Clarice saw the expression on my face. I ran out of the delivery room, man. Apparently, the boy was part of the African-American. I went to the house, packed up. While I was talking about where I could go, I got a phone call. The doctor was ready to take my DNA and compare it to the twins. I got a twinge of 'just to be sure' and I decided to be right there. I was going back to the hospital. Clarice was in bed with a child on one side and a child on the other. She's been crying. "It was the male stripper at the Bachelorette Party. I was intoxicated and some of the girls gave them blowjobs. I was so turned on by his big penis that I dropped my panties and turned around so that he could take me from behind."

"You mean the reason you were so wet that night was because I was getting sloppy for a few seconds?"

"Yeah, I'm so ashamed of myself."

"But did I think that Geneva was watching after you?"

"Oh, I think I said I didn't do anything that she didn't do. She and her husband are still in marriage counselling. Please don't tell anyone."

"Well, I guess I'm supposed to stay long enough to see that you can make it all right at home. It'll take that long to get the DNA testing done."

"You 're not going to stay here? Look at these lovely kids. They need a good dad. Why can't you be that dad?"

"Because I don't think they were made with my sperm.

"Then get the hell out. I'm going to make it without you, bitch.

I left. I've taken a few more days to decide where to go. My landlady's apartment was open, smaller but cheaper. One ride to the apartment and one to the storage room. This is one of those instances where karma was supposed to be of my advantage and have my boss offer me a position in another state. There's no such luck. He said I was lucky enough to keep the job I had.

I received a phone call from the doctor. I assumed it was going to tell me that Clarice was ready to go home. They said that she had already gone home. The call was for the DNA check. The doctor said he normally gave the results in person, but he was about to leave for two weeks, and I thought I wanted the results before that. Duh! Duh!

I jumped on the gun and asked, "Are they mine or anyone else?"

He replied, "Well, yes and no."

"What the hell? Sorry, please clarify it."

"As you know, they 're brotherly twins. It's very rare, but some brotherly twins have different fathers. It means that the sperm of two men was inserted into the mother's womb at about the same time. The only ones I've seen before were in the case of a gangrape. You 're the girl's father. I don't have the matching DNA of the boy's father."

"Thanks." It was worth getting drunk.

I called Clarice, but she didn't answer the question. I was calling her mother. She said Clarice was going to stay there again. My first reaction was, "How convenient it was for Darren." She told Clarice to get on the phone.

"The Rick?"

"Clarice, I just received a call from a DNA doctor."

She was crying, "Me, too. What are we going to do?"

"It seems to me you've got two options. Put the boy up for adoption, and we'll keep the child, or you'll keep both of them, and I'll send as much money as I can."

"I can't give away my son. Why can't you accept him as well?"

"He's not my son. I'm not going to raise another man's son."

"Rick, if I had been married when we first met, and had been the only parent of a young boy, would you not have married me? Wouldn't you have embraced both of us? Legally, then you would have raised another man's child. I'm not going to give up my child."

"But you wouldn't have been married to me when you had another guy with your wife. I'm not going to play hypothetical games. I think you've chosen that time. I'm going to apply child support to the kid.."

"Her name is Eleanor, and his name is Jacob."

"I will add child care and visits to the settlement for Elaine, but not for Jacob."

She hung up, man.

I had made sure that Elaine's birth certificate had my name as father and Jacob's unknown parent.

Clarice and her baby moved in with her mother indefinitely. Darren took off to places unknown to him. Her mother said that her favourite dildo added more than

Darren did. I have visited every time I've been scheduled. Elaine and I were bonded, and she typically cried out when I left. Jacob cried out, too, because his sister was crying.

As Elaine grew older, the number of things we could do together increased. I tried to take her out a few times, and I had to tell Jacob that we couldn't take him. He called out, "Daddy, take me." He broke his heart and mine, too, but I wouldn't give in. I told him that I wasn't his dad, so I couldn't take him away. When they were almost four, Elaine asked me why her brother couldn't come with us. Ok, I asked her why. She wasn't buying it.

"If Jacob can't go, I'm not going." No amount of negotiation or bribing worked. She was as stubborn as her dad. I left alone in tears.

The visitations resumed with me only going to Clarice and her mother's home. At the same time, I conceded to play with both Elaine and Jacob. A new routine was put in place, and I began to get comfortable with the structure. Cue Murphy.

Clarice became seriously ill and had to undergo an emergency hysterectomy. She wasn't on my health plan, so she wasn't able to pay her own. Her mother had no emergency funds and had begun to show signs of early onset dementia. While in the hospital, Clarice agreed to put Jacob in custody and asked me to take primary custody of Elaine. I decided only on the condition that Elaine would be returned to her whenever she felt able to do so.

Physical recovery, the emotional decline of her mother, and her overall sadness for having to give Jacob up for adoption, all took a toll on Clarice. I took Elaine a lot, but I wondered if the sad partings were worse for both of them than staying away. I came to the conclusion that if something had not happened, Clarice would die too soon. I prayed more than I've ever had before. I have a response.

Three months later, I was scheduled to take Elaine on a visit. Clarice looked like death had warmed up. She was a solid 30 pounds lighter than we were when we were married. For a minute, I asked her to take care of Elaine. I was going to have a fast order to run. When I came back, Clarice took some food from her mother, and Elaine played in the living room. Elaine started crying and yelling when I got in. Clarice came into the living room, looked at me and fainted.

When she got there, she looked up at two faces: Elaine and Jacob. She cried and hugged both of them with all the strength she had. Clarice looked at me and said, "How?"

"Jacob was adopted, and I got permission to bring him over. I thought you 'd like to see him."

"Yeah, Rick, that's the nicest thing you could have done for me. Thank you . Thank you. Come here, Jacob, and let me see how much you've grown."

I stayed behind and let the three of them catch up. After a while, Clarice asked, "How long are his new parents going to let him visit me today?"

"I don't know. Let me call." I dialled a number. The phone of Clarice went off. She replied.

I said, "I understand that you want to know how long Jacob will live. It's up to you."

By now Clarice had caught up with her. "You? How could you pull it off? Yeah, Rick's going to mean that we ...." She jumped into my arms and flooded my face. "I love you, even though you are the meanest son of a bitch in the world."

"Language, mama. Language." We laughed at Elaine.

"I kept thinking about the time you asked me if I would have welcomed a child of yours if we had married after you had left the father. I kept remembering that I should have. I would have raised that child as my own and not thought twice about it. Until I realized what a hypocrite I was, I checked with social services. He was a special needs child, and I was bi-racial, so I got quick tracked into being accepted for adoption. Today is his first day as my son. Well, we still have to go to court to make this official. When I picked him up at the state adoption agency, the worker there asked Jacob who I was. He said, "That's my daddy. He's Elaine 's dad, too.

We all cried out and started to make plans. I think Clarice ate more than she had in a week that night. Everything about her improved quickly. Her doctor was pleasantly surprised at her next check-up and removed her from several medications. It was not long before we developed a new routine for the five of us. My boss was fired, and I got promoted to his position. This allowed Clarice to stay at home to take care of her mother while the twins were in school. In a couple of years, Clarice's mother died.

Clarice and I took a moment alone after the funeral. "Oh, baby, there are just four of us now. It's time for you to pick a reward for yourself. What would you want to do, Clarice, if you could do anything?"

"Other than correcting some bonehead mistakes earlier in my life, there's only one thing I don't want — another child."

"But you've had a hysterectomy, you can't have another child."

"You didn't even have a uterus, so you had to have a child. We should adopt another child."

"I've got a big concern about doing that."

"Which is?"

"Just one of them?"

Murphy — Go and suck an egg.

The First Time

Kate woke up as the sun rose early in the morning. She yawned as she sat up in her bed, stretching her arms. Today was the day, it had to be right? She swung her legs over the edge and got to her feet. She walked over to her mirror and looked at her reflection. 5'3, petite but big breasted with long brown hair. She was naturally gorgeous, yet she'd never been with anyone before. She had grown up in a fairly strict religious household, so she had never dared to bring anyone home, lest they feel her father's wrath. But now it was different, she had moved out a year ago and was living on her own. She had her own apartment, her own job, and her own life. Nobody could tell her what to do anymore.

She'd gone through puberty like any other girl, her hormones flowed through her body. She'd done a little experimenting with herself and masturbation with whatever privacy she could get. Yet something deep inside her burned for something else, she wanted…no, she needed to have a man inside her. She picked up her phone from her charger and downloaded the tinder app.

Hopefully someone will be willing to sleep with me, she thought to herself as she set up a profile.

It didn't take more than a couple of minutes before she had matched with a handful of guys. She had some casual back and forth chats with people before being blunt and telling them she was a virgin. She settled on a nice looking Caucasian male named James. He had brown hair, a muscular physique, and was tall. They messaged back and forth for a while before setting a time and a date to meet up.

Okay, see you then, she texted him as she turned off her phone.

Kate gave out a huge sigh of relief. That hadn't been nearly as bad as she had imagined. She felt bad for people who were actually looking for a relationship, surely that was much harder.

She took off her nightgown and turned on her shower, placing a hand under the running water to wait for it to get up to a proper temperature. As she stepped underneath the water she closed her eyes and imagined James running his hands all over her body. She cupped her breasts with both of her hands and moaned as she massaged them, pinching her nipples slightly as she did. She wanted to be perfect for tonight, so she washed her hair thoroughly and scrubbed every inch of her body twice. She shaved perfectly making sure she was smooth everywhere, including the most important area, then turned off the shower.

As she dried herself off she looked in the mirror. She wasn't bad looking was she? Hopefully he didn't think so. She didn't have much experience with dating or standards of appearance.

She put her hair up to dry and patted herself down as she walked to her closet. She picked out a pretty red dress she'd been saving from her senior year in high school. She'd never gotten to wear it, but at least she had it. She laughed quietly to herself.

Picking out a matching pair of lace boyshorts, she pulled them on and set them on her hips. She looked at the pretty red dress. She could have dressed more casual, but he'd invited her to a pretty upscale hotel in the city. Maybe she was under-dressing for the occasion. She was pretty sure he wouldn't complain at all.

Kate pulled the dress up her slender body and zipped it up in the back. She did some light makeup before taking a deep breath. Now came the real question, flats or heels? She hesitated for a second before deciding on a pair of red heels she'd bought to match the dress. With one final check she was ready to go. She got her keys, hopped in her car, and drove to the hotel.

As soon as she pulled in front of the hotel her eyes went wide with admiration. It was far more marvelous than anything she had anticipated. The structure was at least twenty stories tall and adorned in large glass windows all the way up to its sides. She got out of her car and handed her keys to the valet who stared at her awe.

"Pretty amazing isn't it?" he said as he got in her car.

"Yeah, it's really something else. I didn't even know stuff like this existed," she replied as the valet drove off.

She walked up the steps to where a greeter opened the door for her. "Thank you," she said and smiled warmly.

"Have a good evening madam," he said, then smiled back, motioning her through. She walked up the front desk and patiently waited for the receptionist.

A handsome man spoke up. "Good evening miss, do you have a reservation here?"

"Yes, my last name is Lawrence, the first name is Kate. I'm supposed to be meeting someone named James Rogers here tonight," she replied.

"Ah yes, he checked in a few minutes ago. Here's a copy of your room key," he said as he handed her a key card. "You'll be up in room 503."

Kate smiled and took the card. "Thank you for your help."

She walked over to the elevators and pressed the button for Floor 5. She waited patiently until the ding signaled the elevator and the doors opened for her. As she got into the elevator and pressed button 5. She shifted nervously, smoothing out her dress one last time. The elevator stopped on the fifth floor and she walked down the hallway, stopping at the designated room. She took a deep breath and slid her key card in.

The lock clicked and she turned the handle to enter the room. Looking out the window was who she assumed was Jason, he turned around to face her and smiled. He looked exactly like his profile pictures. Tall, clean-cut, muscular, and very…very handsome. Despite being quite attractive herself she instantly felt insecure about her looks.

"You're gorgeous," he said. "I'm almost speechless."

Kate blushed at the compliment and replied meekly, "You're not bad looking yourself."

"Thanks," he replied.

There was an awkward silence for a few seconds before James spoke up. "Are you really a virgin? There's no way with someone as pretty as you."

Kate wasn't sure whether to take that as a compliment or an insult and replied somewhat taken aback. "Excuse me? What's that supposed to mean?"

James stumbled with his words realizing how that came across, "Oh, I just meant that you're so gorgeous, you could have any man you wanted. I'm just kind of surprised that you've never been with anyone at all. The personal reason, or religious, or…?"

"Ah well, I'm flattered. I grew up in a pretty strict family so I never had the chance. Now I'm out in the real world by myself so…here we are," she said and smiled shyly.

James smiled back and there were another few seconds of awkward silence between the two. James finally took the initiative and stepped in towards Kate, placing both of his hands on her hips. He looked down at her soft blue eyes and leaned in for a kiss. Kate looked up at him and gently pecked him on the lips. They leaned their foreheads against each other and smiled. She wrapped both of her arms around his neck and he placed an arm around her lower back. He gently cradled the back of her head with his other arm and pulled her in close for another kiss. The two of them locked lips passionately and kissed each other deeply. They tilted their heads slightly and James moved his hand down from Kate's lower back and gave her ass a slight squeeze.

Kate smiled into her kiss and moved both of her arms to James's shirt. She slowly unbuttoned the top one and worked her way down until it was open down the middle. She pulled it down his arms, revealing his well-toned body. James reached behind her and gently pinched the zipper between his fingers and slowly started pulling it down, making sure to read Kate's response as he did. She started to breathe a little faster but he assured her with, "It'll be okay."

He unzipped it to the end, stopping at her waist, then stepped back. She let the dress fall down her waist and onto the ground, revealing her petite waist but ample DD cups. She blushed red and covered her breasts with an arm out of habit. "You're perfect. I've never seen someone so beautiful in my life," he said.

Kate couldn't think of anything to say. After a second she responded, "You don't have to lie to me."

James unzipped his pants and let them drop to the floor before stepping out of them. "I'm not lying, otherwise I wouldn't be getting undressed for you right now."

He moved over to her and positioned himself behind her. He placed both of his hands on her hips and pulled her close, she could feel the bulge in his boxers pressing against her lower back. He kissed her on the neck warmly and she moaned as a shiver ran through her spine. She looked up at him and both kissed again from over her shoulder. He moved his hands from her waist up to her breasts. Kate reluctantly moved her arm away from covering them, letting them drop free.

James cupped both of her full breasts one in each hand and firmly massaged them. Kate placed her hands over his and moaned at the sensations running through her body. The feeling was so foreign to her, but one thing was for certain, it felt amazing. He pinched her nipples with his hands softly and she squeaked. James stopped for a second to make sure she was okay.

"No, don't stop, I just didn't realize how…sensitive I'd be," she cooed softly.

James continued massaging her breasts for a minute before moving his right hand down her abdomen and to her panties. He traced his index finger along the inner seam of the waistband playfully, then pulled it back out. Without much warning, he fully cupped her mound with his right hand and gave a firm squeeze. Kate's knees instantly crossed as a warm sensation ran through her pelvic region and into her pussy.

"How does that feel?" he whispered in her ear.

"It...it's amazing," she said.

He cupped her mound firmly and used his middle and ring finger to massage the outside of her opening, creating pressure against it. Kate moaned quietly, blushing as she did, but unable to control herself at the sensations running throughout her body. James moved his hand to the waistline of her panties again and pulled them down, revealing her smooth, virgin pussy. She blushed again as no man had ever seen her fully exposed, but he again comforted her. "You're the best catch I've ever had."

This made her feel safe and she grabbed both of her breasts fully with both her hands. She started to massage them herself James used his two fingers to trace lines along her outer lips.

He moved his hand slowly to her clit then gently touched it with his middle finger, sending a pulse throughout her entire body. She moaned loudly and grabbed her breasts. He gently massaged her clit in small circles with his middle finger for a few seconds, making her moan in pleasure. He kissed her neck and nibbled gently on it as he did so, slowly moving faster and faster.

Kate began to feel pressure building behind her pelvis as the familiar feeling of orgasm approached. "D...don't stop," she whimpered. James kept rubbing her clit as she squeaked, "Ah, ah, ah."

Her breaths became faster and more shallow until an orgasm crashed into her body and her legs buckled from under her. James used his strong physique to help hold her body up as wave after wave of pleasure slammed into her. Her pussy muscles contracted as James relentlessly massaged her swollen clit, causing her to gasp. Eventually he slowed down and so did her breathing. He pushed his two fingers inside her for a brief second and spread her juices around her outer lips.

He turned her to face him and picked her up gently in his arms. She wrapped her legs around his waist and her arms around his neck as he carried her to the bed.

He laid her down on the bed, her juices dripping from her soaking wet pussy. He climbed on top of her and kissed her neck softly. He kissed down her body, moving from her neck to her collar. He licked her right nipple with his tongue, then took it in his mouth and sucked softly. He used the right hand to play with her left breast as he rolled her nipple around between his fingers with one hand and his tongue with the other.

Kate moaned happily as small ripples of pleasure shot through her chest down to her waist and back up to her brain. He kissed down her stomach to her v-line and licked a long line up both sides. He moved down once more to her tight pussy and licked her clit directly, making her squirm. He placed both hands on her thighs and went down on her, licking her clit softly at first, but quickly picking up his pace. He thirstily drank up her juices, licking from near her anus all the way up to her clit.

He took her clit in his mouth and sucked gently, tracing small circles around her pearl with his tongue. She moaned loudly as he used a free hand to stick his middle finger inside her. He navigated his middle finger around her insides, feeling the walls of her soft folds then stuck his ring finger in as well. He made a 'come hither' motion with his two fingers and pulled on her g-spot.

Kate's eyes rolled back in her head as he massaged her g-spot with his hand and her clit with his tongue. He started to move faster and faster as her clit and the pressure behind her g-spot began to swell.

"W…wait," she cried as she felt herself about to cum. She placed her hand on his head and went to push him off of herself, but he gripped her thighs firmly and held her down as he continued to stimulate her sensitive parts. "I…I'm going to cum…"

Her words were cut off by her orgasming again, squirting juices onto the bed and into James's mouth. She blushed bright red and began to apologize as he slowly moved off of her, licking his lips. "I'm sorry I tried to…"

He held a finger to her lips and moved his body on top of hers. He pecked her on the lips and then slid his boxers off, revealing an adequate 6 or so inch cock. He placed it against her opening and Kate began to breathe fast again. He rubbed it against her outer lips, lubricating his tip before pressing against her opening. He started to push inside slowly, moving his cock in and out. He pushed a little bit deeper each time until his tip entered her fully. Kate gasped as he pushed himself further inside her. She moaned as her virgin pussy gripped his cock tightly.

"You feel so good," he grunted as he started to thrust in and out of her. She wrapped her arms around his neck and pulled him close as he thrust in and out of her, building up his pace quickly. Before long he was pounding her tight pussy as she moaned with each thrust. Pressure started to build up behind James' pelvic wall and his balls began to contract. Kate could feel his cock growing stiff as she also neared another orgasm.

She let out one last loud moan as her pussy contracted, a powerful orgasm hit her for the last time. James's cock throbbed and spasmed as he shot a huge load of cum deep inside her virgin pussy. He shot load after a load of cum in her before he took a deep breath. Both James and Kate breathed heavily as they came down from their orgasms. He slowly pulled his cock out, letting his cum drip out of Kate's tight hole. She smiled as she got up, the cum dripping down her inner thighs.

"I hope that wasn't too disappointing for your first time," James said.

"It's the best I've ever had." Kate winked.

The Little Girl

If there was something that Anne could be sure about, it was the fact that Peter enjoyed power. Even more so than power, Peter liked to be in total control of every little detail that surrounded him; power such as the consequence of working hard to keep things in sync. She noticed it months after their work relationship had started, though the signs were clear from the beginning if Anne dared to admit. The youngest daughter of Louis and Gabrielle, Anne was twenty-five when she started working for the huge Light Pink Entertainment company, joining the team of executive assistants who were meant to follow the instructions of Peter Berry. All kinds of stories about this man had reached Anne's ears by the time she stepped into the office on her first day, unaware that she would get to prove one, or two of them, to be certain.

Anne had worked as an assistant before, but Peter was the first leadership figure that she witnessed coming out of his office to greet the rookies. Most of the group of new assistants, herself included, received this gesture as a demonstration of kindness and manners from their new boss, but now that Anne had a chance to look back and reflect upon the matter, she curved her lips with a knowing smile. Peter was only keeping things under control like he was used to doing with most, if not every, corner of his life.

"Good morning, ladies," he said with a charming smile, standing very close to Anne's old desk. Mr. Berry was trying to cover most of the space with his gaze, so he wasn't facing her at the moment. From that privileged position, Anne could take a note of his broad shoulders and the little threads of silver tangled in his dark hair. "I hope you find yourselves comfortable in your new seats. I personally ordered them yesterday morning in a rush. It's clear I needed not one, but a whole group of assistants."

The girls were quick to laugh at Peter's joke, and Anne found herself chuckling wholeheartedly. The tension that had filled the room as soon as Peter walked into their shared office was starting to die down, making Anne and the rest of the girls relax behind their desks. There were five of them. Silvia, the woman who hired them, had hinted that they were going to be separated in the future, each one of them sent to a different department.

"I wish you all much success," Peter continued, taking a couple of steps back. He ended up touching Anne's desk with his lower back and, much to her surprise, he didn't hesitate to take a seat on top of the wooden desk. "You already know where my office is if you have any questions." Peter took a pause to smile, scanning the room with his blue eyes. Anne was the last one to be touched by his gaze. They were still making eye contact when he added, "I'm sure you'll be spending plenty of time in there anyway."

Mr. Berry was married. He'd been married for ten years now, and he was the loving father of five-year-old twins that were as blonde as he was. Anne saw the kids once when they came to the building with his mother on a surprise visit. Some of the rumors she'd heard around the time she got hired were that her boss's wife was a cheater. Mr. Berry spent a lot of time away from home, thanks to the business trips that he was forced to take at least twice a year. No one could tell for sure whether Peter was informed about this or not, but it looked like he wasn't. Even when he spent most of his days pacing around the office with a focused look on his face, his charming smile made a comeback every time Elizabeth walked past the elevator doors.

Anne thought of it as understandable. Peter's wife was stunning. Light brown hair, tall and lean, she had the range to be the First Lady of a wealthy country, and together with Peter and their kids, they looked like a family straight out of a postcard, even if Anne's boss wasn't the type of man you would see and think of as physically attractive. He wasn't as tall as other men and he wasn't bulky either; Peter was broad-shouldered and thin, a figure that matched very well with the suits he chose to wear for work. Anne's first thought about him was elegant. Peter carried himself with an aura of authority and classiness that was beautifully intimidating.

"What are you thinking about?" Mr. Berry asked her, dragging her out of her thoughts.

Anne's smile got wider, accentuating the effect of her red lips, her boss's favorite color. That was a classical Peter question. Anne was sure that it was one of those corners of his life that he liked to keep under control, but there were aspects of her that were still out of his reach, like her thoughts and the decisions she made. She'd learned to pay close attention to him, not because she wanted to use this information in any way, but because she found Peter fascinating at times.

They were driving towards the house that Mr. Berry had rented for their stay in Tokyo. It was the first time that Anne had traveled abroad, and she'd insisted they were going to have enough room in a hotel, and that an entire house wasn't necessary. She could tell that Peter was prone to overspend, especially when he wanted to impress someone. It was both flattering and mortifying for Anne to find that her boss was trying to impress her.

Peter sealed the deal claiming they were going to have enough room for sure, but not enough privacy. And he wanted to fuck her in every corner of a large house, the biggest one he could find, so there was no valid argument that Anne could use to fight him.

The house was hidden in the middle of the woods, so there were miles of trees ahead. Anne's gaze got lost in the wilderness. The green walls placed on each side of the road made her olive skin stand out, but she wasn't focused on her reflection in the rear-view mirror.

"I was thinking about your family," she admitted, licking her lips. Peter squinted at her answer as if trying to figure out what she meant by that. Anne was sure her words had to take him by surprise.

"My family?" he repeated slowly, careful not to take his eyes off the road. Back in the place where they rented the car that Peter was driving now, one of the clerks had warned them about the possibility of having animals crossing the pavement from out of nowhere. There was a pause before he asked again, with an air of amusement this time, "Why are we thinking about my family?"

"I don't know," Anne replied in all due honesty since she wasn't sure about the point of revisiting her memories about Peter's kids at this point. It wasn't like she was feeling guilty now, right? "I was remembering that morning at the office when Elizabeth brought the children with her and you were so happy to see them. You were always so happy to see them, even if she dropped by on her own. It was curious to me because, back then …"

Anne stopped herself before she could continue to speak without thinking. She realized all of a sudden that there was always the possibility of Peter not knowing about his wife's affairs, and she felt terrified to reveal something painful to him while they were supposed to have fun during this trip. It was still a business trip, but Peter had insisted Anne to tag along with him because, lately, "he needed her to survive," as he had joked out loud at the office. Half of the staff knew they were fucking, and Peter liked to feed the masses by making those sorts of comments out loud. He enjoyed the way Anne got all shy and flustered when he did it.

"Back then?" Mr. Berry repeated as he'd been waiting patiently for her to continue.

Anne took a deep breath, then shifted in her seat. She glanced at his phone's screen, showing the route they were following, and she was relieved to find they were only twenty minutes away from the house. After taking a pause, Anne decided to be honest.

"There was this rumor when I got hired," she said slowly, taking her time to pronounce each word, "that Elizabeth was cheating on you."

Anne was afraid to be dropping a bomb in the middle of the car, but Peter took a couple of seconds to analyze her words and then he started laughing. The woman raised her eyebrows in surprise, laughing along with him in a nervous demeanor. For a moment, she thought Peter was laughing because he found the whole rumor thing to be ridiculous, but he was quick to prove her wrong.

"I know, I probably started that rumor myself," he admitted, shrugging carelessly. Anne straightened her back in her seat as she gave Peter a judging stare, asking for an explanation. Mr. Berry chuckled again. "I mean, it wasn't like I did it on purpose. I talked about this with someone at the office, someone I thought I could trust, but they ended up spreading it everywhere."

"So, was she really cheating on you?" Anne asked him with a frown.

The light in Peter's face dropped for a bit, proof that the topic was not as funny as he was trying to make it pass. Anne spied on his phone again and noticed there were only ten minutes left. It'd been two years since the last time she saw the twins in person. For a minute, Anne wondered what it would feel like to grow up in their skin, realizing years later that their mother was hooking up with the gardener while Dad wasn't home, because he was fucking his secretary in Tokyo.

"It's complicated," Peter finally said.

He took a turn when the GPS advised him to do so, and they were able to spot the house at the end of the dirt road. The man started driving real slowly then, since it was even more likely that an animal would show up from out of nowhere during this bit of the trip.

"Elizabeth and I are friends. We haven't been a couple since the twins were three, more or less."

"Do the kids know? That you two are not together anymore?"

When she received nothing but silence from his part, Anne knew that she'd crossed a boundary by talking about his kids. The look on his face reminded her of the Peter he was during most of his business meetings; the intimidating entity that was both hard to decipher and confront.

Anne had decided to pursue this type of job to learn a thing or two about management before climbing the ladder herself, but people like Mr. Berry weren't a part of her plans. She hadn't considered the possibility of feeling sexually attracted to her boss, let alone having her boss reciprocating those types of desires.

Was it a mistake coming to Tokyo with him? Anne wasn't sure yet.

She jumped out of the car without saying a word and followed Peter in silence into the house. The place was big enough to host at least ten people, but they were going to be using only one room. For sleeping, at least. Last night, when she pictured what traveling with him would be like, Anne had daydreamed about Peter and she walking into the house, tangled in the middle of a deep kiss that ended with them walking half-naked towards the kitchen. She could see the kitchen now, untouched and bathed by sunlight, and couldn't help but think that she'd ruined their affair before it had even started.

*

Anne woke up in the middle of the night to the sound of footsteps, and she immediately sat up in her bed, covering herself with a blanket. She squinted at the open door, the only source of light at the moment, and she was able to tell that Peter was standing at the threshold with something in his hands.

"Thank God, I thought you were gone," he said, and the tone in his voice let Anne know that he was smiling.

She chuckled.

"What are you talking about?" Anne inquired.

She'd fallen asleep a couple of hours ago after Mr. Berry had knocked on her door to announce that he was going to get some groceries. He didn't try to ask her to come with him, but Anne replied that she was tired and preferred to stay in bed anyway. Peter claimed to be okay with this, and he closed the door without saying anything else.

"You're a box of surprises sometimes, Annie," Peter replied, dragging the woman by her feet towards the edge of the bed. Anne gasped, sitting up straight when Mr.

Berry pushed her up with a hand pressed at the back of her neck. She looked up at him as she realized that he was carrying several ties. "I was picking a bag of apples when it hit me that you could be faking a headache to get the hell out of this house."

Half-asleep still, Anne chuckled once more while she closed her eyes for a moment. She was having a hard time deciding whether this was real or not. She thought Peter was going to act distant for the rest of the trip; the woman surely wasn't expecting him to show up in her room with mild anxiety about her leaving. While Anne reflected on this, Mr. Berry pulled her arms up, holding them together in front of her face as he started tying her wrists with one of the ties.

"What are you doing now?" Anne asked him, her eyes finally opening wide.

It was Peter who was a box full of surprises. The shift in the situation was waking Anne up for good, and she was both relieved and curious about Mr. Berry's skills when it came to knots. The fabric of ties was being tightly wrapped around her skin. It would've looked beautiful as a decoration, but there was something darkly erotic behind it all that was making Anne's lower belly sink with desire.

"I'm making sure you don't leave in the middle of the night," Peter answered in a whisper, kneeling in front of her to perform the same trick around her legs.

Anne tested the strength of the leashes around her arms and wasn't surprised to find that she couldn't force herself free. A delicious chill went up to her spine. Peter had been joking around with tying her up anytime, but she never thought they would manage to do it so soon. Not like this.

"How are you planning to fuck me if you're tying my legs together?"

Anne gasped a second later, taken by surprise by Peter's move. He was resting on top of her arms now, her breasts pressed against the ties that Mr. Berry proudly wore to work. The skirt of her nightgown had been pushed over her back, revealing her ass for Peter to see. The woman gasped again when her boss spanked one of her cheeks, closing a fist in her chocolate brown hair in order to pull her head up with a fine grasp.

"Don't underestimate me, Annie," Peter's words were dragged out one after another, and they had an immediate effect between his assistant's legs.

He gently pushed Anne's underwear down until her panties were wrapped around her thighs, and she was able to feel how the anticipation was building up in her crotch. She gasped once again, enjoying the tickling sensation invading her pussy. Peter pushed her hips upwards with one hand, clearly refusing to let go of her hair.

Anne became suddenly aware of her lack of control during this encounter. She licked her lips, biting the bottom one as she moaned; Peter had rewarded her with a new couple of slaps during her epiphany. She could only think of her boss's cock, of how swollen and hard it had to be because this was Peter's favorite scenario. He was in complete control of the situation. The burning sensation in Anne's ass was quickly mixed with the pleasure coming from Mr. Berry's middle finger, making its way inside her soaked entrance.

Anne was begging for it by the time Peter reached her clit. He knew where to strike in order to have his assistant on her knees, though she couldn't comply at the moment, as much as she would've loved to. Anne's face fell over the sheets when Mr. Berry finally let go of her, and she took advantage of the moment to rub her features against the bed, whimpering.

"Please," she begged, tortured under Peter's skillful thumb. He continued to rub her swollen clit in circles, creating rushes of electricity that were exploding onto Anne's legs. She just couldn't stand the heat.

Right when she was about to be struck by lightning, Peter positioned the head of his dick against her burning cunt. He stopped touching her altogether, and Anne was only able to feel the heat that her boss's skin was radiating.

"Peter, please ..." she begged desperately, as she tried to push herself against him.

There was something about having sex with Peter that turned her logic off. She became pure flesh and yearning, always craving for more, wanting to feel every inch of him inside her.

Mr. Berry ended up pleasing her, and Annie got an answer to her question. He was going to fuck her whenever he wanted, as he pleased, whether she was tied up or not. But it was better when she was wrapped in his ties. If there was something to discover that night, it was the fact that she preferred to be under Peter's control.

The Forbidden Sex

I took off my shirt and sat in a chair that was facing the bed, as I was told. Then David walked to the nightstand and flipped out a pair of handcuffs, and soon I did hear a cold metal click as he slipped them on the back of my wrists. It's been my birthday. I was expecting the handcuffs. It was exactly what happened next that I didn't expect.

David and Dena had become close friends with my wife, Julie and I. David was a police officer, so I was wondering if the handcuffs were a department issue. He used to work in the gym, my spouse and I run, but he would always take Dena with him. I don't know if he saw me looking at his wife first, or if he couldn't keep his eyes away from Julie who started it. This way, we soon found that David and Dena had been swingers in the past and that they would swing again if the right couple came along.

Julie and I were a little reluctant at first, but I think it was more out of fear of what the others might feel. Julie couldn't hide the fact that she liked watching David's workouts. He had tight muscles, solid biceps, and she couldn't even move as he came to the register, dripping with sweat. She would fall all over herself to get him a fresh towel. Julie liked that kind of man. That's why she was married to me. I was a professional coach and won my share of amateur bodybuilding contests.

Julie told me that she had fantasized about muscle men like us at her disposal. And she always accepted the fact that I had to support well-toned women who worked at our place yet didn't seem to mind that I've been around with scantily clad women all the time. But when David and Dena became friends and shared their history, we discussed things more thoroughly.

From the beginning, our wives hit it. They were both blond, well toned and tanned. You'd presume they were brothers. And they were going to giggle while David and I were just out of the distance.

So, we learned that they had been with a couple or two of them, but it wasn't "intense" enough to keep the relationship going, whatever that meant. So, Julie and I were giving it a try.

We all had a planned vacation to Madrid happening, it was believed by all of us that this will be one of our best vacation together. Oh Madrid! Madrid!! Holla Madrid!!! We got to HOTEL VILLA MAGNA and booked separate rooms. Deep in us we know a lot will be going down.

We are used to just light romance in front of each other to swapping partners out of each other's sight using separate bedrooms. Since informing one another about our sexual exploits with David and Dena, Julie and I had the most excellent time with each other. Soon we got each other's partner in the same room, and it was exhilarating.

Julie and I were all of a sudden debating issues more frankly than ever before and actually feeling closer to each other. We felt very close to David and Dena, of course. We've learned that they've stopped swinging because they've never been able to find a couple willing to step up the relationship, experiment, and push the excitement. Once the spouses had been swapped, that was it, and no one was willing to take any further step or leap; whatever that meant.

We've enjoyed having sex in the last few months. Julie and I were talking a lot more. I have often seen Dena and Julie giggle in the corner. Soon we wanted to know what they were thinking, because we were a game. What was the next step all about? Next thing I know, it's my birthday, my shirts off, I'm handcuffed and I'm sitting in a chair.

I realized like I was the only one didn't understand what was going on here. Dena and Julie seemed quite relaxed and began to take off their clothing. I was advised that to take the journey to the next stage, I had to do everything I was asked to do and just enjoy it. I agreed to that.

David told the girls to begin the show. Instead Julie bent over and hugged Dena. I saw them naked. I've fucked both of them. But they've never really touched each other in the last few months. I had to admit that it was exciting.

The two naked blondes were writhing on the bed. Their legs were entwined, and their tongues danced in each other's mouth. It was an incredible sight to see my wife in the arms of another woman. My dick was bulging against my pants.

Then it all went dark. David had placed a hood over my head, which scared me at first. But I heard women still humming and slurping in each other's tongues. The sound was soothing, and even though we had never done any kind of bondage, the darkness seemed to intensify the experience.

I noticed my jeans slip off along with my socks. This didn't really bother me that David had pulled my clothing off, but I suddenly felt weak. Handcuffed, hooded and naked; just a few feet in front of me could I hear the sounds of sex. I could hear David undressing his clothes beside me, and then he realized that he was going towards the crowd.

"God, David, you're so brave." I heard my wife say. Then I heard more slurping and more entwining bodies. There were brief moans and a lot of movement in the room.

"Stick your cock to her David, fuck her," Dena said.

I imagined David fucking with my wife, plunging his dick inside her shaved pussy like I'd seen him before. It's just that I've always been able to relieve myself by raping his wife. Dena had quite a small boobs than Julie but they were quite perky, and then when we fucked her, she moaned even louder than Julie. When I heard the screams of sex, I could feel my penis stretching for relief.

Some of the beds squeaked but soon stopped. Then I felt hands on my thighs and long hair brushing my testicles. Another set of hands, then. "Do you want to see what you're missing from?" Dena asked. I did, of course.

Just enough for me to see Dena positioning herself above my dick, David lifted the hood from behind. She spread her legs and slowly lowered herself. But as soon as the tip of my dick touched her pussy, the hood went back over my head, and I heard everyone back on the bed.

The hugging noises go on. More wet sounds, man. More moans, man.

"Oh, Julie, lick the pussy," Dena said.

"David. Damn your dick is a big one." Julie replied.

I could only imagine what they were doing there. There were more groans and breathless pleas. My erection was still straining. My heart was pounding.

"The women make love to each other," David said. "They're gorgeous." Soon the moans stopped and I felt the movement again. Then the hood came up again.

"You might want your own friend. How about that?" Dena said. David was holding up the hood just enough to see Julie dropping herself over my cock with Dena directing my penis into her soaking cunt. As soon as she barely touched her wetness, everything went dark again.

The threesome was having more sex. Then come back to me. More sex and get back to me. I would have touched my cock once. Many moments, they would have let me peek just enough to see one of the girls ' lips licking my penis slightly or enticing me with their cunt, which was pouring out of their threesome anatomy.

My heart was pounding. My cock was stretched. The air in the hood was getting thicker.

"You want some of them? Do you want to visit us?" they would threaten.

So soon as the hood went up, David was holding my cock and pointing it at my wife's mouth. I raise my hands for my cock to touch her wet lips. I was hoping for help. Even David's warm hand felt good, and I begged for a pussy to plunge it into, or at least for David to jack me away. But the hood went back to leave me with the sounds of sex and hardness.

I don't know how long this has been going on, but it seemed like an eternity. I was able to feel the pulse in my dick. I felt like I was going to faint, and my breathing was rapid. My cock was stretched to the sound of sex thinking the salvation was so real but so far away. The noises were silenced again. I began dreading the moments of silence before the hood went up.

"You want it, don't you?" Dena's voice said quietly.

"Yes." I said to him.

"Didn't you hear us fuck each other?" Julie's voice had the same hypnotic tone.

"Yeah." "Are you going to do anything to ease the desire?" Dena said.

"Absolutely," screamed my spirit. I heard soft music that was lustful and hypnotic. The fragrance of incense reached my nose.

"Stand," Dena ordered.

I noticed the slurping did sound on the bed and my spouse softly moaned. I sensed Dena next to me as she led me to the edge of the bed and started rubbing the lotion on my throbbing dick. My hands were still tied and my head still hooded, so I still felt quite helpless hearing only the sounds of my wife squirming on the bed in front of me to the monotonous beat of soft music drooling in the background.

"Do it, sweetheart. Let's do it. Oh, this is so bad." I heard my wife gasp.

I thought that Dena was moving closer to me. Her lips pressed against my ear; her hand was still lubricating my dick, which cried out for relief.

"Do you want to be wicked?" she whispered.

"Yes." I was breathing.

"Then show us that you can be wicked." She snarled, pulling the hood out of my head. My heart was just running. My wife lay down in front of me on her back on the bed. David knelt between her thighs, his butt in the air mere centimeters from my cock, slurping gently at her cunt. Dena reached out his hand and inserted a finger into the ass of her husband. David grumbled. She worked it slowly in and out.

She grabbed the handcuffs behind my back with her other hand, and pushed me towards her husband. My fuckin' ass bumped. She grabbed it and aimed at his puckered hole with my dick and then looked at me with a sultry look.

My wife shrieked with pleasure. David slightly spread out his legs in anticipation. Dena went to study my profile. A weird feeling washed down over me. I just wanted to have sex. I just wanted this couple to have sex. And all of a sudden nothing mattered except sex.

Lust flooded my loins and I arched my hips in the direction of David. Before, I never dreamed of having any urge to fuck a guy. Yet, the age didn't matter. Dena smiled and guided my dick to his opening as I strained to reach his ass.

She rubbed my cock round and smoothing out the lubricant across his ass's puckering. David grumbled. My wife was just moaning. My heart nearly jumped with lust from my mouth. I was pushing forwards.

My penis hit David's butt sphincter; inside, the cock vanished. Slowly I pushed forward and watched my dick sank his way into this man who still enjoyed my wife's wetness. I slightly pulled back then pushed forward again, lubricating the inside of his ass with the lubber on my dick. The lube spread and his ass were now accustomed to my intrusion and relaxed. Soon my dick would slide in and out freely and methodically.

Dena reached behind me, unlocking his handcuffs. I instinctively grabbed my lover's hips, and started fucking him. Dena then crawled to the bed to watch my wife being hugged briefly.

So, it was. No couple could have taken this before. In addition to walking on the wild side, David and Dena wanted to crave the forbidden. So, Julie and I went with them on the voyage. And apparently Julie liked it. And I'll confess, having crossed into the forbidden one; I've always loved it.

David moaned while I was laughing at him. My dick slipped smoothly inside and outside his ass. He couldn't focus on the cunt of my wife anymore so she slid beside him and started to jack him off as we played. I was so hot I knew I weren't going to last long.

The vision was terrific; my naked wife was jacking off David, and Dena fingering nearby. When I grabbed a muscular man's shoulders, his breasts and buttocks were unexpectedly voluptuous to me; tempting even. I always wanted to have my wife; I wanted Lisa and the experience she and David offered most recently. I just wanted it all now. The whole wicked journey and adventure that was about to come. I fucked his gorgeous ass. Julie pulled his dick out of her mouth as she kissed her own already wet cunt, and Dena masturbated frantically beside us.

My cock gleamed with lube as it erupted from his mouth, and was then sucked inside.

His butt had my cock puckered and clenched. He was closer than any motherfucker. Its sphincter seemed to swallow me over and over again. The fire swallowed up my cock. My head had started spinning and my heart was racing.

"David. I'm going to come. God, I'm going to cum inside of you." Julie pleaded, "Fuck him baby, let me see you cum.

Dena continued to gasp; her fingertips were operating on her cunt with vigor. David grumbled louder.

I just felt it. It was like a wave crashing down upon me. My balls clenched. My body was not mine anymore.

"I am cumming... Oh, Fuck... I am..." My voice gave way to inhuman grunts. My body was spasming and my ass's buttocks clenched. For dear life I grasped David's hands and jerked involuntarily. I felt streams of cum gushing out of my dick and flooding its intestines.

David's butt twitched and through the groans I heard something splattering in the bed underneath us. David poured stream into bed after wave of pearly cum, with Julie still pounding his cock. Dena angled her back against her hand, and Julie began more aggressively fingering her own pussy, until both moaned with satisfaction.

Cum began to leak out of David's butt with the last gratification throes that we forced out of those last few strokes. When Julie released it, David had grabbed his own dick and ended up relieving himself. He then collapsed on the bed and I still impaled my dick inside his quivering ass on top of him.

I was unaware of the girls, when I kissed David's neck back. My hips straightened in and out again going to squeeze out another incredible amount of pleasure from his ass. He stretched out his legs to accept the attempt but both of us were spent.

My semen was oozing from David's butt as I removed my cock. To mix with its sticky fluid, it spilled onto the bed. The girls had recovered and showered us with their own kisses. We kept quiet for a while. But we slowly realized this was only the start.

Many people may be repulsed by our actions in Madrid. Some might say this was just a fling. But you did have to be there really. Perhaps we've been mocked over an imaginary line that others won't cross because we knew as we reached it; it's been theoretical all the time and from our own development. Due to this, we all were close and free. I think we have to make our Madrid plan more frequent.

Horny MILF Sex in Public

After being cheated on by my husband and a messy divorce, a great fuck is what I needed. As a college librarian, I see lots of kids in my library, but Luke was exceptional. We admired each other from afar the first week of school until he came up with an excuse to talk to me. We got to talking and ended up having steamy passionate sex in the library after hours. I seduced him, pushing him up against the bookshelves and giving him the blow job of his life. He was incredible and enthusiastic as we fucked. My experience and his passion made for a very hot and satisfying session. It helped me to own my sexuality after my divorce.

As I walked to campus, I could feel the cool of the air in that familiar autumnal way. It was the first day of the new semester. The trees were turning that burnt umber as the leaves began to die, falling to the ground. I was glad that the weather was beginning to change for the better, along with other things in my life.

After a difficult summer riddled with divorce papers, I was looking forward to the school year starting up again. I found out that my husband had been sleeping with his 25-year-old secretary. They had been doing this for a year, I later learned.

One night soon after summer had started, I didn't have much to do and decided to stop by my husband's office to drop off some dinner for him since he had been 'working late' so often. To my dismay, all I found was him ramming his pathetic excuse for a penis into his secretary who was bent over his desk. Needless to say, I filed for divorce soon after that. My whole summer had been spent in anger, frustration, and lawyer's offices.

But the summer was over now, so I could get my life back on track and return to my job as a librarian at the local college. I had spent most of the summer indoors, mourning the loss of my marriage, but the cool of the air felt nice as I walked to campus.

The first week of school, I saw all the usual kids: the juniors and seniors who had spent the last few years frequenting the library, studying and working on projects. As a librarian, I see so many kids coming in and out of the library. I see their study groups, who they hang out with, occasional drama, what kinds of books they check out. I've always liked people-watching and it's a nice way to bide time in the library.

There was one guy who stood out, though. I had never seen him before, so I figured he must be a freshmen or a transfer student. He didn't look like he was eighteen; he looked a little older with his wide shoulders and trimmed beard. He had a nice chiseled jaw and it seemed he had a strong muscular body. I longed to rip off his shirt so that I could take a look at his strong abs and youthful chest. Although I wasn't typically attracted to younger men, I found him very sexy.

Then again, I'd been married for about twenty years and hadn't thought too much about men other than my husband. I had always been satisfied sexually with him, as we had a very healthy sex life. Well, up until he decided I apparently wasn't enough. Since the divorce, though, I hadn't taken a lover. Sure, I had satisfied myself from time to time, but it wasn't quite the same. I'd been feeling horny, and I was getting hornier as time went on. I had been feeling like it might be time to satisfy those needs. My husband, while attentive in bed, had a small dick, and I was looking forward to an upgrade. I wanted a nice big cock to fill my pussy in a way that his never could.

That Thursday night, I decided to draw myself a nice relaxing bath. The first week of school was usually pretty hectic with students asking questions.

Steam rose from the water as I stepped into the bath. I slid down and rested my head back, allowing the warm water to wash over my body. My stomach was covered by the water with my breasts were floating, allowing my nipples to poke out of the water. Admiring my body, I realized that I had avoided looking at my body for quite a while. But I realized that my body is still incredibly sexy despite the years added to it. I was still thin with perfectly large breasts; I still had beautiful wide hips and a pretty pink pussy that was shaved and bare. Loving my body was something I'd nearly forgotten with age and monogamy.

I placed my hands on my breasts and squeezed them, enjoying the feeling of it. My skin was smooth and silky from the bubble bath, allowing my hands to slide easily along my body. I slid them down my tits, feeling my stomach and wide hips, before sliding my hand down between my legs.

I thought about this young man from the library, who I later learned was named Luke, as I steeped in my hot bath. I had noticed that he tended to stay in the library quite late. Since it was a college library, we stayed open until 2AM to allow students who stay up late to study. I found it a little curious that he had been staying that late, though. Since the students' workload had not become so heavy this soon in the semester, not many students were staying so late in the library. Regardless, he was always there when I turned the lights off and on fifteen minutes before the library closes. He would soon stroll out after that, as if he had been waiting for the library to close.

I allowed my knees to fall to either side of the bathtub, as I slipped a finger into my wet pussy, feeling around the soft interior. I sank down deeper into my tub.

I also noticed that he often sat near my librarian's desk and occasionally looked over at me. One time I caught him staring at my cleavage, which was framed nicely by my low-cut dress.

Sliding my finger deeper into my pussy, I started getting turned on. Smiling, I started moving my finger in and out of my pussy, feeling the softness of it as I did so.

I vaguely wondered if he was into older women. It might not be the most ethical thing to date a student, but it's not as if I was a teacher or anything. Not that I was thinking about dating him, but I may have been fantasizing about fucking him a little in the tub. It had been so long since I'd had a nice good fuck, and by his looks he seemed like he would be. He had a muscular body, as if he played sports of some kind, and sexy eyes that contrasted his smooth skin well.

As I thought about him, I imagined him without a shirt on. I slid my fingers out of my pussy, softly brushing over my inner labia as I placed my fingers on my clit, feeling it between my fingers and gasping slightly. Young men were always so eager and horny. It turned me on thinking about him like that. I started slowly rubbing my clit softly in the bathtub, feeling my breasts as I did so. As I started rubbing my clit harder, I thought about how it would be to fuck him. I kept on rubbing harder and harder as I thought about him fucking me hard and fast. I yearned to be fucked like that; I needed it. Water was splashing with my hand moments by the time my back arched in ecstasy. I let out a satisfied moan having climaxed to the thought of this sexy man eagerly fucking me.

The next day, I returned to work at the library in red lipstick and heels. I was feeling a little extra confident from my self-love session. Fridays are usually pretty slow since most kids are out starting their weekend off by getting drunk, fucking each other, or whatever it is they do. So usually there aren't too many kids in the library.

As the night wore on, the few kids in the library started trickling out. Except for Luke. I thought it was a little curious. By one in the morning, there wasn't anyone but him and me in the library. I noticed him get up, browsing through the fiction section. I thought about asking if he needed help finding anything. Yet, I saw that he soon found what he was looking for and approached my desk.

"Hi, I'd like to check this out," he said. I smiled widely with my red lips and took the book from him. He was checking out a copy of Mary Shelley's Frankenstein, a book that I was rather fond of. I smiled at the opportunity to flirt with him. Since last night, I'd been feeling sultry and flirtatious. I'd worn my best dress and silky smooth stockings.

"Mary Shelley," I said, impressed.

"Yeah, it's for my English class," he said as he looked up at me, "It's one of my favorites but I left my copy at home."

"And where's home for you?" I asked, leaning over the desk, which gave him a good view of my breasts pressing together, practically popping out of my dress.

"Minnesota," he said smiling, trying not to look down at my breasts.

"How do you like it here?" I asked, trying to continue the conversation as long as I could. He seemed like he didn't mind. In fact, he seemed to like it, especially the view of my breasts.

"Oh yeah. I mean, I've only been here a couple of weeks," he explained, "I just transferred here."

"I didn't think I'd seen you around," I said, winking and turning to check out and stamp his book.

"I bet you see a lot of kids working here," he said, leaning over the counter to make sure I heard him. It was cute; I looked back at him.

"I do indeed," I said flirtatiously, "What are you doing here so late on a Friday night anyway?" I approached the desk again, meeting his eyes with mine.

"I don't know. I just..." he stuttered, trying to find the right words, "I guess I just didn't have anything else to do tonight." He stared right at me as he said it, looking at me with his beautiful eyes. I felt overpowered by their beauty and his sex appeal.

"Why not?" I said, leaning over the desk to show off my cleavage in my low-cut dress once more. "You're a handsome young man. You should be out with a girl or at a party."

"Oh, I don't know," he said scratching his neck as he tried to find the right words. "College girls always seem so superficial to me."

"Well, what kind of girls do you like?" I flirted, leaning closer.

"I like older women," he said boldly, looking me in the eye having finally mustered up the energy to flirt back.

"Is that right?" I said in a sultry tone. My mind flashed to us fucking against the bookshelves....

"So you like Mary Shelley?" he said, changing the subject but genuinely interested. I appreciated that he was trying to get to know me a bit better. We ended up talking for quite a while about literature. Eventually, we wound up sitting down at one of the tables so that we could continue our conversation more comfortably.

"Oh goodness," I said looking at my watch. Over an hour had passed while we sat there, "We were supposed to close ten minutes ago."

"I guess we got a little carried away," he said, reaching over to touch my hand. The moment our hands touched, I felt myself getting wet for him. I smiled up at him, wrapping my fingers around his strong hand as I leaned closer to him.

"I guess so," I said, adding, "I liked this very much. It's rare that I get to have these kinds of conversations. It's nice to meet someone who shares the same interest. My ex-husband never liked talking about literature with me." Smiling as I said the word ex-husband. He leaned in closer, squeezing my hand. I closed my eyes, letting the pleasure wash over me. When I opened my eyes, he was looking at me wantonly.

"I'd better go lock the doors," I said, letting go of his hand and gliding over to the entrance to lock it. I turned back around, and walked back towards him. I felt sexy, confident and powerful. I walked right up to him, putting my hand on his chest.

"Ms. Preston..."

"Call me Maria," I said. As I pressed my lips against his, he hesitantly grabbed my waist. He kissed me back soft and passionately. His wet mouth on mine, he ran his hand up my back while pulling me closer to him. I could tell that he was a little reluctant. Surely he was wondering if this was okay to be making out the librarian and it was likely that he was intimidated by an older woman.

As he kissed me, I felt like a young woman giddy with sexual energy. I forgot about my ex-husband completely, allowing myself the pleasure of this moment. He kissed me softly at first, feeling my soft lower lip between his, gently nibbling on it. I felt liberated and I wanted to continue this. I kissed him harder and more passionately, creeping my tongue into his mouth as he did the same. His passion was growing, but he was still a little unsure.

"Is this okay?" he said, pulling back. I just smiled devilishly in my red dress and took his hand, leading him so that we were in between bookshelves. That way if anyone were to walk past the library, they wouldn't see us. (Besides, who hasn't fantasized about fucking against a bookshelf in a library?) Pushing him up against the bookshelves, I kissed him hard and passionately. With both my hands on his chest, I moved one slowly down, feeling his hard muscles as I did so. My hand was on his crotch; I could feel his firm cock pressed up against his jeans, practically begging to be let out.

My expert hands unzipped his pants without a second thought. I teased him a little bit, brushing my fingers along his boxers where his cock was. I could feel it get harder as I did so, the way his muscles contracted, bouncing his dick up into my hand. After teasing it a little, I grabbed it tightly in my hand. He gasped, looking up along the shelves.

Smiling, I took this as my cue to get on my knees. My face was close to his cock, just inches away, as I admired how thick and long it was. It was so hard and veiny; it turned me on to see his big cock so hard for me. I wrapped my fingers tightly around the base of his cock before teasing him with my tongue. I gently licked the tip, sending him into a world of pleasure. Then I licked his cock from base to tip with a wide, hard tongue. He moaned in ecstasy.

I wrapped my red lips around the head, letting him feel my warm, wet mouth, my tongue swirling around his sensitive tip. I liked to start slow so that the good stuff feels so much better. Most young men forget this part, but I could teach him. I teased his cock like that for a little while, just licking the head. I allowed my soft wet mouth to lightly run over his shaft until he was moaning so hard like he couldn't take it anymore.

It was then that I plunged his dick into my throat for the first time. I stuck it in nice and deep so that my mouth was at the base. Pulling my head back, I sucked hard on his head and ran my hand along his shaft in beat with my sucking. My expert tongue was massaging his cock as I did so, fluttering along his shaft as it went in and out of my mouth.

I looked up at him to see his face contorted with pleasure as he was trying hard not to make too much noise. I always loved seeing that look and knowing that I'm doing my job right. My pussy had been getting wet this whole time, but I could feel it getting even wetter as I was giving him pleasure. I plunged his cock deep down into my throat while contracting my throat muscles to massage the head of his dick.

"Oh god," he moaned, "Where did you learn to do that?"

"Practice," I said slyly, after letting his dick fall out of my mouth, a line of saliva connecting my mouth to it still. He took the chance to grab me, lifting me up to meet his face.

"You are amazing," he said, looking me in the eyes.

"I know," I said, pushing him back again and getting ready to get back on my knees, but he stopped me. He pushed me back this time so that my back was against the bookshelf while he kissed me as hard as his push. I turned me on to be controlled like that, pushed around in a sexual way.

Continuing to kiss me, he slid his hand into my bra feeling up my bare tit. I moaned from the pleasure as he rolled my nipple between his thumb and forefinger. By this point, my nipples were hard as rocks.

With his other hand, he slid my dress up, running his hand along my soft thigh. He looked down at my sheer thigh-high stockings, pleasantly surprised. He slid his hand along my inside of my thigh and then started rubbing my crotch, which was wet enough to have soaked through my panties. I moaned at his touch. He bent over to slide my panties off. Stepping out of them, I wondered what he would do next.

He lifted my leg up so that it was next to his hip, still feeling my wet pussy. Slipping a finger into me, he rubbed all around my wet pussy. He moved his fingers up to my clit, rubbing it nice and hard. I could feel waves of pleasure flowing through my body from getting even wetter.

With his other hand, he took his member which was still wet with saliva. He began rubbing it up and down, jerking himself off rapidly and making his cock harder. He reached into his pocket, taking a condom out of his wallet and rolling it onto his penis. I could feel my chest getting flushed from the excitement.

With my leg still up, he rubbed the tip of his cock along my inner labia, sending me into a small fit of moaning. Suddenly, he plunged his thick cock deep into my pussy, filling up my wet snatch. I gasped; I hadn't felt this for months and it had been driving me crazy. I could feel how much thicker his dick was than my husband's. He was slipping it in and out of me which allowed me to feel the ridge of the head rubbing against me, stimulating me more and more.

He started out slow, the way I like, moving in and out of me slowly and then getting deeper, hitting the back wall of my tight pussy. I loved a cock nice and deep inside of me; I'd almost forgotten what it felt like to be fucked like this.

I may have been a little on the older side, but my pussy was still as tight as ever. I did my Kegels every day, so I had a lot of control over my vaginal muscles. I squeezed his thick cock with my muscles. It was something he had probably never felt before sleeping with young women who often didn't have these kinds of pussy powers. It sent him moaning, so I began doing it even more, massaging his cock with the inside of my cunt. He stopped humping me momentarily, allowing the unique massage wash over him in waves of pleasure.

With the realization that he had stopped fucking me, he started up again, faster and deeper this time, desperately wanting to pleasure both of us. He was hitting me in so many of the right spots, making my pussy feel full as it was tightly engulfing his cock.

He quickly lifted up my other leg, so that my pussy was spread wide for him and my leg wasn't in the way. My back was pushed up hard against the shelves as his strong arms held tightly onto me. He was vigorously fucking me, his cock getting harder inside of me and my pussy just getting wetter. I was surprised with his swiftness and strength; it made me hot that he could take control of my body in that way.

Seeing how turned on I was and hearing how hard I was moaning, he started kissing my neck and nibbling on my ear. I gasped, turning my face away so that he could kiss and suck on my neck better. He ran his tongue along my neck and up to my earlobe to suck and pull on it with his teeth. The sensation was incredible, making my pussy contract without my even meaning to. I could feel the wetness building up inside of me, filling me up along with his cock.

I could feel how deep he was pushing his cock into me; it felt so good. I loved a nice thick cock deep in me. I had been missing it for years, being with my ex whose cock was pathetic compared to Luke's (whose name I had gotten from his student ID when he checked out his book). It occurred to me that I wouldn't even know his name if not for that, which made me hot.

He started fucking me fast, as deep as he could. I started moaning; it felt so good to be fucked like that. It had been years since I was fucked this good and I was feeling like I was about to cum. The way he was fucking me was getting more and more intense until I finally exploded.

I hadn't had an orgasm like that in so long. I could feel it in my whole body as my pussy started contracting like crazy on his girthy cock.

"Fuck, I'm fucking cumming. Fuck me, fuck me, fuck me!" I yelled, wanting more. He started fucking me harder and deeper and faster as I was screaming. I was pumping my hips into him the best I could at this angle, which made it so much more intense.

"You like that?" he said.

"Oh God, yes, please keep doing that," I said, and he did. I could feel myself climaxing again as he pumped his thick meat into me over and over again.

Suddenly, he lifted me up still inside of me, holding onto my legs and brought me over to lay me down on one of the desks. He started fucking me there, still standing up. The desk was the perfect height for his cock to slip into my pink pussy. I lifted my legs so that they were resting on his shoulders. It made it feel like he was even deeper inside of me than I had imagined. I moaned, enjoying the new position.

As he fucked me, I arched my back which put more pressure on his member. He was pulling in and out of me to tease me a little. He pulled all the way out and then rammed his dick deep into my pussy over and over again. Then he started passionately fucking me hard and fast, digging his hands into my soft hips.

"Oh god… god… yes. Fuck yes. Oh god, I'm cumming," he moaned, face contorted with pleasure. He let his breath out sharply as he held his cock deep inside of me. I started flexing my Kegal muscles again, milking the cum out of his cock.

"That feels so good," he groaned. I just smiled, pleased with my work. He bent over me so that we were semi-cuddling as his cock was still inside of me. I could feel his hard muscular body pressed against my soft breasts. He kissed me gently and passionately. Our mouths were wet for each other and he kissed me sloppily as he sucked on my bottom lip.

He suddenly lifted himself up and got down on his knees. Luke began feasting upon my pretty pink pussy, admiring it as he did so. My pussy was still wet as he ran his tongue up and down on my clit, moving it in circles and making me moan. I'd forgotten how good that felt, and he was superb at it. He started with his tongue soft, licking my clit like a little kitty cat, before tonguing my pussy hard, putting pressure on my hard clit. It sent shivers all through my whole body.

He smiled up at me, as if asking if I approved. I smiled back at him, moaning and groaning in pleasure. I was already extra-sensitive from cumming twice, so it didn't take long for me to climax again. The sensations built up quickly, sending me into a hot fit of ecstasy that was better than the last one. I grabbed his hair to let him know he was doing his job right, moving his head up and down gently as I pleased. I looked down at him, letting go of his hair. He looked back up at me, saw my satisfied face, and smiled, climbing back onto the desk next to me.

"That was amazing," I panted, exhausted. He kissed me.

"It really was," he said, "I haven't had sex that good in… ever. You're really good."

"That's what happens with years of practice," I said, smiling at him. I ran my finger along his chest, toying with his hair and saying, "You weren't so bad yourself."

"I doubt that," he said laughing, "I'm not nearly as experienced as you are." He looked over at me, admiring my beauty and sexual prowess. I took his face in my hand, pulling it close to me to kiss his sweet lips. He may not have been as experienced as I was, but he was enthusiastic and passionate due to his youth.

"I don't mind," I purred, "You're still the best fuck I've had in a long time. Besides, fucking older men doesn't mean that they're going to be good at what they're doing," I added, giggling. He smiled at me and cuddled his head between my neck and shoulder. I rested my head against his, glowing with orgasmic bliss.

"Do you think maybe we could hang out outside the library some time?" he asked innocently.

"I would really like that," I said, "Maybe you can come over to my place sometime." Smiling and drawing my body closer to his, I thought of all the fun we could have in my bed, all the different ways he could fuck me.

"I like you," he told me, "I've been admiring you since I first laid eyes on you."

"I was wondering why you've been staying in the library so late," I teased, flattered.

"I've been working up the courage to have an excuse to talk to you," he said shyly. "I never thought this would happen, though."

"Well, I sure hadn't planned on it," I said, laughing. "But it felt so right," I said more seriously. It really had; I hardly even thought about it as I first kissed him because it felt so natural. It felt like it was meant to happen, like this was the universe's way of helping me get over my divorce.

After that night, we started seeing each other often. His youth helped me to feel younger as well. I had taken control of my sexuality and it was empowering. I had been held down by a man for so long, it was satisfying to explore my newfound sexuality.

The Orchid and the Heat

Adrenalin rushed through her veins as Vanessa lay there on her bed impatiently and eagerly waiting for a response. This might, at last, be it. A part of her mind was restless, absolutely stressed out, thinking about whether this was what she truly needed, yet the perverted part of her mind screamed with the passionate realization that this was it. Her entire body was shivering as she felt a tingling effect in between her legs; she envisioned what it would feel like. The waiting was intensely severe. Following a few moments, she couldn't help herself. She required total relief.

Cautiously unzipping her pants, she slipped her hand underneath the pink fabric of her panties and let out a peaceful groan as her chilled fingertips touched her burning and yearning clit. As soon as she sensed the welcome and immense relief she had been yearning for, it was hampered by the sound of a message coming through on her phone.

"Yes!!! x"

A wave of ecstatic enjoyment gushed through Vanessa. This had been very nearly a year in the making. It had all begun when Alicia had knocked on her front door to introduce herself and get acquainted with her. That was the first day in college and they were freshers. As the door opened, Vanessa recalled how fast and within moments she fumbled with words, as if something was caught in her throat. Alicia was really an extreme stunner.

Her skin was radiant like a brilliant golden brown. Her hair streamed down in silky dark sheets from her head, stopping at a point which, had she been stripped, would have elegantly canvassed her succulent bosoms in a way that it would make Vanessa go wild. She was in her Levis and a striped tube top, flaunting her impeccably flat and sexy stomach. As Vanessa's eyes ascended this young lady's sexy body, she turned out to be deliberately mindful that she was trying to figure out if she was a C or a D cup and felt a jolt of guilt as she understood how shocking this must look. Alicia, clearly, had not taken any note. She had just giggled and made that tempting curve on her lips wide and said "Howdy. I'm Alicia. I'm in the room across the corridor. I've quite recently moved all my stuff in, yet there's nothing else to do. Wanna chill with a beer?"

It had taken Vanessa embarrassingly long to acknowledge what she had implied; however, the minute she did so, there was nothing except to say yes. Vanessa couldn't resist being in wonder of the natural and extraordinary confidence this young girl radiated. She could never have just made friends by asking a stranger to go for a beer.

They had spent the rest of the day together, going for another couple of beer cans, and got along amazingly well. They were so like-minded (criminal psychology), they enjoyed the same food and above all (for Vanessa) they were both somewhat nerdy. She didn't know why but she had believed it best to conceal her obsession with The Game of Thrones and Star Trek. However, that had flown out of the window the minute Alicia, who absolutely had none of those concerns, had started to make references to them.

When Vanessa had got into bed, she hadn't understood what to think. She had kinky fantasies about sexy and attractive girls previously, everybody did now and again, yet she'd never felt like this about a girl. Now she wondered if she'd felt or never felt like this about anybody. Every one of those worries was pushed out of her head when she started to envision what Alicia would resemble bare and naked and what things they may do together. Before she could realize, her hand was in her panties and she was moistened vigorously than she had ever been. That night was simply the first time when she had tasted her own excitement, her own ecstasies. She thought, on the off chance that she truly liked young girls, then she should like the taste herself first. She had taken her fingers out her pants (groaning a little at the loss of sensational relief) and gradually touched the dribbling fingertips to her lip.

It was astounding. The taste was salty, a bit warm. She licked her hand dry and kept on stroking off. At the point when her climax was done, she lay there for some time more. She had needed to change the bed covers before retarding to sleep. They were completely soaked.

That year had been so special, so very amazing. She went through pretty much consistently with Alicia and every night, wondering about her. Be that as it may, after she came, she generally had a guilty feeling. She realized she would never have the sheer confidence and truthfulness to confess anything. Besides, Alicia was certainly a straightforward girl.

Neither of them had returned home over the summer. From the very minute, Alicia had said that she was staying so that she could work and save some money over the Holidays Vanessa had discovered some flimsy reason to stay back with her. She just craved to be around her.

Then, just seven days back, they'd been chilling out over a drink when Vanessa was courageous to ask her friend, completely out of the blue, if she had ever wondered about young girls.

"In that way, you mean to say?" Alicia had chuckled.

"You know precisely what way, and what I mean," replied Vanessa, not expressing too much enthusiasm over her friend's teasing.

Vanessa had been overjoyed to hear what Alicia would reveal to her next. Not just had she considered it, wondered about it, Alicia gave detailed depictions of the perverse dreams she had.

"In any case, I've never gotten the opportunity to give one a shot," Alicia replied grinning mischievously.

It had not come up once more. Not until today. Not until, in a moment of mental courage, Vanessa had informed her.

"Hello, Alicia. I realize this is somewhat odd, however, I've been thinking... how desperately would you like to fulfill those twisted fantasies of yours"

She had waited hours for a proper reply from her.

"...a lot..."

Vanessa had almost screamed.

"Would you like to come over at this point?"

Then was the reply that made it final.

"Yes!!! x"

Without waiting any further for a knock, Vanessa proceeded to open the front door.

There she was. She was wearing a similar top as that at first time. Similar Levis jeans. They gazed their reflections for a minute in each other's eye with passion and amazement. Vanessa was so desperate to suck on that brilliant dark-colored golden skin.

Before they could realize it, they were kissing passionately. It was quick and wet and hot. Vanessa pulled her best friend inside. Alicia ran her hands through Vanessa's long blonde hair and drove her down onto the bed. Her hands felt their way around Vanessa's succulent bosoms and as she bit down on her friend's pale neck, it left a red imprint. Love bites, they always mark lovers passionately for one another. Vanessa groaned as the object of all her savage wants and wild desires shook all over her, moving gradually to and fro kissing her, fast and wet and hot.

She flipped Alicia over and, proceeding to kiss her, moved her hand down into her panties. Her fingers whirled in her friend's juices as she groaned wildly as if being exorcized. Alicia nearly whimpered when the fingers were pulled back and, now trickling with cum, Vanessa once again licked her fingers dry.

"Fuck foreplay, I have to taste you," said Alicia and now the ball was in Vanessa's court to groan with wild wants. Her pants were being pulled off. Her panties were gone instantly. Before she could realize it, Alicia was grinning up at her from between her legs.

She nearly screamed as the moisture of her companion's tongue got together with the burning moisture between her legs. It was the quickest she had ever cum in her life and this time she really screamed. It resembled the alleviation of 19 years of sexual tension.

Similarly, as her legs quit shaking, a tongue returned in her mouth. She could taste herself the other young girl.

"Fuck these clothes," said Alicia and she slid out of her top. The remainder of her clothes rapidly followed and there she was. Standing completely naked before Vanessa, she was so flawless, so provocative, so attractive. Vanessa stood up and kissed her. Alicia drove her back onto the bed. Vanessa put her leg under in the beginning, their clits simply caressing each other, but then quicker and in a little while, they were both groaning so wildly and savagely.

At that point, Vanessa shifted once more and with no time her tongue was inside her friend, Alicia's .She tasted incredibly awesome.

They kept on fucking longer until Alicia's cum had drenched Vanessa's face. They eased each other over and over for quite a long time, never wanting it to end, never getting tired. It was quick and wet and hot.

In the long run , the two lay alongside one another gasping. "That was stunning," the two of them said simultaneously, and chuckled, and kissed. They lay next to one another and finally fell asleep.

When Vanessa woke up the following morning, she was wrapped in the arms of her new darling. She could, in any case, smell their sweat and cum from the last night. She realized that when Alicia woke up it would start once more. She couldn't have cared less on the off chance that she was gay or not. All she knew was that she adored her, and she cherished fucking her and she needed to continue fucking her for whatever length of time that she could. This was the beginning of her new life.

A Sex Club

When I placed a personal ad in the San Diego Reader ten years ago, I was looking for a wife. I was twenty-four and didn't know all of the things I wanted in a woman; however, just one date with Juliette was all it took for me to realize that I had found an amazing woman. Now, many years later, I'm still married to Juliette and our relationship grows richer and more interesting as the years pass.

We share many interests: the love of traveling, trying new restaurants, watching documentaries and foreign films, and browsing bookstores. If this was all we did together, I'd feel pretty lucky. Juliette's wild side, however, captured my heart. We have perused adult bookstores, tried new sex toys, gotten lap dances at topless clubs, and tried new sexual techniques and positions. Once Juliette turned thirty-five, she became even more willing to try new things and push me past boundaries I thought I'd never cross.

The only thing I've wanted to do that Juliette's been reluctant to try is attending a swinger's club. Not because she didn't think it would be fun having sex in front of other people, but because she was worried that the clubs would be unsafe or that there would be hard drugs and rough people.

2001 was a traumatic year for Juliette. Her mother died in August after a six-month fight with cancer, and then the attacks of September 11th... After these events, Juliette decided we should take advantage of the time we have together and try things we wouldn't ordinarily have considered. Around December, she began hinting that she was interested in going to a sex club if I'd take her. After some research online, I found a local club that had a Couple's Night once a month. Juliette and I looked over the Power Exchange's website and decided we'd attend one of their "couple's" events. I was ecstatic and had trouble concentrating at work.

On the drive up to the club, we talked about everything except where we were going. After parking in front of the club, I looked over to Juliette and noticed she was quiet and no longer smiling.

"What's wrong?" I asked.

"I'm not feeling comfortable about this. We can stay 20 minutes and I'm definitely not taking off any clothing." Knowing that arguing with her would only make her want to go home, I acknowledged that we'd leave whenever she wanted.

Juliette wore a tight pair of Diesel jeans that accentuated her shapely legs and her tight fitting black turtleneck showed off her firm breasts. I was very lucky to be out with a woman who I found so damned hot.

I paid the $40 admission fee and began wandering around. We started off in the main room where there was a man fucking a bored-looking brunette doggy-style. The buff and tan guy wore a Chippendale-style bow tie and was fucking the disinterested looking woman. The stud smiled and looked around the room and seemed to think he was something special, but we found him to be more of an interesting spectacle than arousing. Every few minutes he would take a break and stand up and stroke his cock to the music while the woman remained on all fours talking to a friend of hers who was standing near the stage. Instead of being horrified, Juliette found this couples antics amusing.

"Al, look at how he thrusts that dildo in her ass while he fucks her. Will you try that on me sometime?" It did look like that had potential to please as the brunette finally perked up a little bit when he began driving both his cock and the dildo into her. Her friend got on the stage and took over the dildo duty so that the guy could fuck her without a distraction.

We got up and wandered around again and made our way downstairs where we sat down and watched two men getting blowjobs from their girlfriends while a third woman kissed each of the other women's breasts. The hallway was dark and there were too many onlookers blocking our view of the action so Juliette sat down on my lap and began kissing me. After a while, we wandered back upstairs to the main room where the dude was still banging his girl for what had to have been more than 90 minutes. Juliette declared that the woman should get a medal for endurance.

"You know Hubby, this is a lot different than I expected; I'm actually getting kind of turned on watching these couples screw. I'm willing to give you a blowjob if you want. How about finding a room where you want it?"

The date was turning out better than I ever imagined. I grabbed my wife's hand and walked through both floors of the club trying to find a good spot for my blowjob.

After passing through the jail cells, dungeon chambers, USMC Recruiting room, and medieval banquet hall, I decided on the pool table in the main room as it was well lighted, lots of people around and not claustrophobic.

When we got to the main room, it was nearly deserted so I climbed on the pool table and removed my shirt, laying it out to provide some cushioning on the table as I knew I was going to be on it for a while. I couldn't help but think how lucky I was getting a blowjob from my sexy, redheaded wife.

Juliette got up on top of me and firmly pushed me down and began kissing me. She thrust her tongue into my mouth and sucked my lips into her mouth.

"Hubby, I'm getting so fucking wet. I can't wait to suck your cock," she told me as she pulled off my boxers and fondled my cock. With one hand, she cupped my balls while with the other, she rhythmically stroked my cock with light caresses. She teased me by alternating between rubbing my cock and then rubbing her hands up my chest. During all of this, she stared into my eyes with a look of love and lust; her green eyes never leaving my eyes. Juliette gave me another ear-to-ear smile before sucking my cock into her mouth. People started gathering around to see my expert cocksucker of a wife give me one of my most memorable blowjobs. With slow, deliberate movements, Juliette licked from the base of my cock to the tip, and then engulfed my entire cock in her mouth. Juliette continued this wonderful torment a few more times and then asked, "Do you want me to give you a blowjob with my shirt on or off?" This was more than I ever could have asked for. "Take your top off so that I can play with your tits". Juliette grinned and pulled off her turtleneck and unsnapped her bra. Now topless, she sucked my cock back into her mouth.

Prolonging the blowjob and my pleasure, Juliette took frequent breaks from sucking my cock and would kiss me on the lips until she judged that I had come down from the edge of orgasm. I could tell she was getting very turned on as she continued grinding her pussy against my thigh. I didn't want to push my luck and pull down her pants, so I slid my hands under her jeans and massaged her ass. Juliette started sucking on my cock again and pushed a finger up against my asshole. I know she really wanted to finger my ass, but we'd forgotten to pick up the lube packets they had in a big bowl at the front desk. In any case, the pressure against the base of my balls and ass felt great and it wasn't going to take long for me to come in her mouth.

Every now and then I'd pull my focus from the world where Juliette was enthusiastically sucking my cock and would look around to see a crowd of people staring at us. At one point, I glanced up and looked at an attractive blonde woman less than a yard away who was smiling at me. It struck me that this was the first time anyone had seen Juliette or me doing something we had always considered so private.

"Juliette, I'm about to come!" I moaned as she quickened her pace. I came in her mouth as her saliva-slickened lips continued to glide smoothly over my cock. I was oblivious to what was going on around me as I arched my back in pleasure, my toes curling as my orgasm rolled through my body. Too soon, my orgasm came to an end and I relaxed and sunk back down to enjoy the feeling of Juliette's mouth tightly wrapped around my cock. Normally, Juliette is a spitter, but this time she swallowed all of my come and continued to suckle my cock. Then moving up to my mouth, she give me a salty, come-filled kiss and told me how much she loved me. It melts my heart when Juliette kisses me after a blowjob; I feel so intimate with her and love the feeling of her on top of me after giving me such pleasure. Her wet lips and talented tongue quickly got me hard again. Unfortunately, we weren't up for another round at 1am on a Friday evening.

Juliette grabbed her juice bottle and took what she humorously calls a "cum-chaser" and smiled at me while I slowly got up and got dressed. Juliette put her shirt back on, but not before I gave each nipple a little kiss. I realized that my amazing night out with my wife was coming to an end as we gathered our stuff together. On the drive home, Juliette joked that she was surprised that I could perform in front of so many people. "You are such a gifted cocksucker, how could I have failed to come?" I replied.

I smiled all the way home. Had we actually performed in front of a bunch of strangers? We were both somewhat giddy as this was definitely the wildest thing we had ever done.

Tired, but still exhilarated, we arrived home at 130am and quickly went to sleep. I had a wonderful evening and was thankful I had such a fun wife to share my life with.

I awoke around 8 AM and recalled with disbelief the previous night. I was so horny thinking about our evening at the Power Exchange that I was about to get out of bed, sneak into the guest room, and play with my cock as I imagined getting another one of Juliette's blowjob. Juliette is normally a late riser, but she began stirring and snuggled up against me and moved her hips in a way that I knew she was awake and turned on.

"I'm still sooo turned on from last night. I can't wait 'til we go back," she told me as she swung a leg over me, allowing me to feel her damp pussy against my thigh.

I wrapped my arms around her while she continued describing what we should do at our next visit to the club.

"Hubby, I'd love it if we can go back and make good use of the pool table. I want to get naked with you and 69 you on that table so bad."

While she was telling me this, I envisioned Juliette on top of me, her pussy inches from my face and her legs around my head as she sucked my cock. I love sixty-nine with her, as there are so many sensations to arouse me -- licking her clit and burying my face in her wet muff as she reaches forward and sucks my balls into her mouth. Not to mention the warm feeling of her breasts against my tummy as she wiggles her bottom all over my face.

Having Juliette's soft body pressed up against me while she told me how she wanted to be fucked in public quickly gave me a throbbing erection. I leaned over and gently swirled my tongue around each of her nipples.

"Al, do you remember what that Chippendale-wannabe was doing to that woman last night? Remember how he was playing with that toy in her ass? You can either ram a butt plug in my ass while fucking me doggy style or you can butt fuck me while shoving a dildo in my cunt. So which is it going to be?"

Such a dilemma: Invade her ass with a butt plug or my cock? After the exquisite blowjob she gave me at the club, I figured a suitable payback would be filling her pussy with my cock while pleasuring her ass with the butt plug.

I kissed my way down from her soft, pink nipples to her pussy and was delighted to feel and taste Juliette's wetness. My fingers slid easily into her slick pussy and I could feel her strong muscles as she clamped down on my fingers. She was so wet that I was able to slide several fingers into her cunt at once.

"Hubby, please kiss me."

"Kiss you where?" I replied, knowing full well what she wanted.

"You know where."

"Yes, but I want you to tell me"

"Kiss my pussy! Lick me and make me feel good", she finally asked.

I stuck my tongue in her opening and was rewarded with a taste of her tangy juices. I very much love licking Juliette to orgasm, but I was going to tease her a little since she was in a mood where she wanted to have an orgasm while I fucked her.

Diving on Juliette's red-haired muff is a favorite way of pleasing my wife. I gradually ran my tongue from her opening to her clit and then pulled her clit up between my lips. After a few minutes of sucking on her clit, I began kissing the inside of her thighs, slowly working from the point behind her knee to almost her pussy and then brushing my face teasingly close across her muff to start kissing her other thigh where I would work my way back to the slick folds of her cunt.

Time passed quickly as I cuddled between my wife's legs and tried my hardest to please her. Juliette moved her hips around so that she could position herself where my tongue could do the most good. Every now and then, she would raise her hips up high so that my tongue gently grazed against her light pink anus. Sensing that she was beginning to get really aroused, I inserted my finger into her cunt and pressed and rubbed her spongy G-spot while rapidly tonguing her engorged clit.

"Fuck me now", she pleaded. Juliette rolled over and got on all fours at the edge of the bed, shamelessly wiggling her shapely ass. I got off the bed and stood behind her, savoring the view of my wife's creamy skin and aroused sex. I put my cock up to her slit and in a single stroke, slid my cock in until my stomach was pressed firmly against her ass. The pleasure was intense as I gently stroked my cock into my wife while I gently rubbed my hands over her soft bottom. Juliette gave me some extra thrills as she used her strong pussy to clamp down on my cock.

"Oh, you have such a hot body, Juliette"

"Please get the butt plug and fill me up like that woman on stage last night", she pleaded.

I quickly retrieved the butt plug from our toy drawer and ran back to my aroused wife to find her busy frigging her clit.

"Finger me. Finger me like you were doing before", she demanded.

Fingering her pussy as she asked, I began running my tongue gently around her asshole.

Every now and then when Juliette gives me a blowjob, she treats me to the wonderful sensations of a rimjob; alternating between sucking my cock and rimming my ass. Now it was my turn to return the favor as I spread the cheeks of her bottom and lightly licked around her tight hole. Her moans of pleasure became louder as I flicked my tongue around her ass while I fingered her pussy. As she got more turned on, I began working my tongue harder into her ass. She reached back and spread her cheeks for me so that I could lick and kiss her to my hearts content. As I rimmed her, I ground my cock into the sheets and was getting close to orgasm from just licking her. Not wanting to come, I got up and lubed the small, pink butt plug and gave her one last lick from her clit to the base of her spine before gently working the plug into her ass. Little by little I inserted it. I'd pull it out a bit, squirt more lube on it, and then move it deeper into her ass until it was fully inserted. Once her ass was filled, I thrust my cock into her pussy while slowly twisting and pulling at the butt plug.

"You sound like you really like the plug in your ass," I asked as I ground the plug into her ass.

"Oh that feels so damned good", she yelled. "Ram that dildo in my ass. Ram it hard. Oh that is so fucking good. I feel so full with you cock in my pussy and the plug filling my ass."

"Do you think that you need a bigger plug now that you're used to my fat cock in your ass?"

"Yes. Oh yes." came her excited response.

The dirty talk pushed both of us to orgasm. When she came, she fell forward on the bed and I tried to remain still for a minute to let her enjoy her orgasm and to recover so that she could continue for her second orgasm. After a few moments, we scooted forward in the bed so that she could stretch out and get ready for some more thrusting. I moved my legs to the outside of hers so that I was straddling her lower body while she got to squeeze her legs together making her pussy even tighter around my cock. Pumping my cock into her, I intentionally ground the butt plug into her ass with my pubic bone. Juliette started moaning again and I knew she was close to another orgasm. I too was close to coming -- the feeling her soft ass up against my tummy and the extraordinary feeling of my cock in her cunt was too much to contain.

"Juliette, you feel so good" I whispered into her ear as I felt the tightness of an approaching orgasm. Within minutes we both came -- Juliette yelling loud enough to wake our neighbors and me with a quiet, yet intense orgasm. We remained joined for another minute or two and then I reluctantly withdrew my cock and slowly pulled out the butt plug.

"Juliette, you are such an incredible fuck", I told her as I lay down next to her. "Al, I never thought getting fucked in the ass would feel so good." She looked at me and gave me a blissful look and kissed me and then said with a grin, "I'm getting that strap-on from Good Vibrations and I'm going to butt fuck you to show you how damned good it feels."

"You keep promising", I replied as Juliette has been promising this on and off for several years.

"Well, I'm going to suck you until you are hard. Get you in the missionary position and drive a large plastic cock in your ass while I use both of my hands to stroke your lubed up cock."

"And then what?" I asked, wanting to hear more of her sexy scenario.

"Oooh, I can see you are getting hard just thinking about it!" she told me as she began sliding her hand over my hardening cock.

"I'm getting really wet thinking about watching you spew your cum all over yourself while I fuck you and play with your cock. You aren't going to turn that down, now are you?"

"Juliette, anything you want," I replied. With her husky just-fucked voice, she made it sound good enough to try.

Juliette wants to go back to the Power Exchange soon, but this time we will do some serious 69'ing and fucking on that pool table.

The City of Lust

Damn, I am horny. I forget how not having sexual intercourse on a regular basis makes me feel. Irritable, crabby, stressed. However, I guess I should have thought about this before I awakened with Ted. He had been fairly useless for many items, but that guy needed a libido like a randy adolescent. Well, if I cannot have sex, I could also get the job done. I am able to forget about my needy pussy for a while once I am in the library, immersed in my study project.

Until that sexy, delicious hunk using all the tight t-shirt walks beyond and makes my knees go weak.

What the hell is a gorgeous young thing like this doing functioning in the reference part of this library? Here, amidst the matronly girls with their shapeless dresses and tired eyes. He is a breath of fresh air for my exhausted lungs. Oh great, somebody needs help using the backup machine. He comes out of his desk, and I get a glimpse of his toned upper chest. If I lean a little to one side, then I could see his extended legs also. Nice.

Studly this is an additional bit of bonus to hanging out in the library. I adore this place! Only the smell of all of these publications makes my heart glow. I have always loved to see, and with a place where I could go and fill a bag with a prized treasure which does not cost me a dime is my idea of paradise.

I frequently have a rest between customers, so that I have the chance to work in my endeavours within this tranquil haven. I hang on the next floor since it is silent, though now somebody is singing along with whatever app he sees on the computer. But that is okay, I am happy also, let him sing. Although I attempt to concentrate on the monitor in front of me, my eyes have been attracted to Studly. I subtly have a look at his bum as he walks past. It seems good.

He is a little thinner than I like my guys, but what's moving and toned nicely. His buzz cut reminds me of a military man, and listening with him help patrons. I could tell he is smart and individual. Possibly a little too mild-mannered to maintain my ardent soul interested for the future, but great for a quick romp. I have been grinning at him for many weeks now, saying goodbye and hello. No ring onto his finger; however, that does not mean anything nowadays. Because he is not reacting to my flirtation, I must assume he is either gay or quite devoted.

I mean, come on, who wouldn't want ME? Focus, concentrate, kind! I slide in my earbuds and then pull a new-age channel on Web radio.

There. Now maybe my thoughts will remain in place, rather than go off to la-la-lust-land. So I'm I in my job (now!) I lose track of time, and I startled when I feel a tap on my arm.

"We will be closing soon, ma'am,"

Studly informs me. Ma'am. I am not a ma'am; my mom is a ma'am. Well, perhaps I really do look like one now, along with my hair up in a bun and my comfy jacket on. It is chilly in here. Still, I feel as though he has thrown down a gauntlet, and I am not one to run out of a challenge. There is nobody on this floor except both people, and a couple of minutes until closing time. I saunter over to the desk and clear my throat.

"Excuse me, do you help me with something?"

I ask. The kind soul he is, he's grinning as he climbs out of his desk, not glaring in my way the women downstairs do once I request aid. I direct him back to some secluded corner and standing behind him reach as much as some top-shelf. I push my body near him, very shut, leaving no doubt it's a deliberate move. There is no time to be coy today.

"I cannot quite reach this novel,"

I shout in his ear. I do not move as he gradually stretches his arm to catch the publication, then turns out. He attempts to back up; however, there is not any place to move. He reflexively hands the book to me, confusion on his face.

"We are closing in only a bit,"

he says, taking a tentative step to one side. I follow along with our bodies touching.

"You understand; I do not believe I understand your name. I'm Trixie."

That is a lie, obviously. I give an enjoyable, fake title when I am poor. "I'm Josh," he stammers and eventually looks into my eyes. "Hello, Josh. I wonder, have you got a couple of minutes to help me with something different?" I track my finger down his torso, then splay my palms flat

On his belly. Damn, the sense of a tough, body. Moisture types between my thighs.

"I, I am visiting somebody, they operate here also..." he starts.

"That is okay; I do not need a telephone or a ring or a dedication. I only need a little time with you nude. Ask her to join us."

Oh, where did this come from? How bold of me. But what the hell, yet another stylish, tight, young body from the combination could be fun. She was likely one of these adorable little things that function from the children's part. We'd dismiss her thoughts, both people performing her once.

"You are available to a threesome?" Josh grins, along with a flare of fire sparks in his eyes. Sure, why not I would share. There is lots of Josh to go around. He whips out his phone and sends a fast text. These children, so quickly with their palms. I really hope they move slower. He flips a switch to dim the lights; therefore just a few sunbeams light our shadowed corner.

Perfect. "While we are waiting," he trails two fingers beginning at my temple, down my cheek, tracing my collar bone down to my own breast. Rubbing the protruding nipple brings a moan from deep inside my throat.

"You are so beautiful. I have been observing you. I can tell from how you move you are a hot-blooded girl."

Ah, now I am a 'woman'. Much better. The ding of the elevator disturbs us. Josh peers from our hidden nook and grins. "Now, the actual fun begins. "A blonde Viking strides.

A man Viking. Um, what? "Trixie, this is Theo, he functions in the books-on-tape section. They keep away him, and that means you most likely don't see him a lot." Hell no, I suppose maybe not.

I would remember if I watched this gorgeous hunk of a man. What was happening here? Librarians were assumed to be both old and frumpy, maybe not sexy and hot. "That is 'somebody'?"

I request Josh, though everyone can see from the goofy grin he is madly in love with Theo.

"But wait, if you are gay..."

"We are a tiny whatever, sweet Trixie,"

Theo says using a British accent which sends chills down my spine. He slowly removes his belt. "We simply love sex, and we like to perform with. How about you?"

My heart skips a beat as his belt thuds into the ground. I have been with two guys. Can I be able to take care of this? They continue to undress, and condoms drop just like candies out of Theo's pocket. I stand with my mouth hanging open. My very own personal strip show.

Theo obviously spends a while at the fitness centre, though Josh is toned and in great shape also. Well, well. My sweet, cute dream man has become a powerful stallion, finish with a ferocious hard-on.

Theo is prepared for action also, by the looks of the stiff tool. My temperature soars and today, not only am I bloated between my thighs, drops of sweat have shaped between my breasts. I pull my shirt over my head, grateful I wore a rather bra now. Josh grabs out a stool and perches onto it.

"Theo, catch a few books for Trixie to stand. That is, it, today, only bring your beautiful self-facing me, straddle my thighs..."

As I spread my thighs facing Josh, Theo reaches under my skirt and pulls my panties down.

I measure them out, enjoying the rush of cool air that strikes my pussy lips. Josh lifts up my skirt around my waist, pulls my buttocks in towards him and impales my entire body on his cock that was hard. We moan collectively. Such bliss, to really have a good bit of man inside me.

I gasp as Theo's fingers probe my asshole. "I really don't know if I could fit you. I really don't do that too frequently," I inform him.

"I will go nice and simple. I attracted a pat of butter out of our break space to slick up you."

His finger slides right into my back hole, and I automatically clench my pussy. Josh unfastens my bra and lowers his head to suck on my breast.

Entirely obsessed with the hot and tingly sensations coming out of my nipple, I unwind as Theo rubs the head of his penis around my hole, then slides it all of the ways into my buttocks. He starts to move gradually, softly stroking in and out. Josh soon picks up the rhythm and the three people stone together.

Theo and Josh caress each other and me, palms everywhere.

Possessing both openings stuffed, and a tough, sweaty body in my front and back would be like dancing with a storm: thunder and lightning, power construction. A statement blares on the speaker, interrupting our bliss.

Five minutes until closure. Much as I'd prefer this to go on forever, I understand we will need to wrap this up. I place myself just directly on Josh, rubbing my clit against his pubic bone. My shouts escalate in quantity, and both guys pick up the speed. With a yelp of delight, I arch my back and come back.

Theo follows fast with a stifled groan, and Josh is right behind him, throwing his head back as he lets out a shout. The ding of the elevator causes us to freeze. What a beautiful, motionless tableau we have to create, I believe. Is somebody going to see this sensual spectacle?

"Josh? You about here?" A voice calls.

"Just finishing up with a patron. I will be down in just two minutes."

"Okay. See you shortly." Another ding and we breathe a sigh of relief, then immediately collect our clothes and apparel.

"Sorry, that was so rapid, love. Others prefer to get out of this on time. Could we have you for a suitable dinner and much more fun in our location shortly?" Theo asks. He strokes Josh's cheek. "This is a great chef and enjoys to show off his culinary abilities."

I sigh with envy. One day, I would have somebody look at me like this, eyes beaming with love. Until then, I could bask in the overflow ardour of both of these beautiful men.

"Sure, I would prefer that. Home cooking is obviously the very best." We exchange phone numbers and emails and go our individual ways. My body and head hum thankfully, and that I reflect again what a superb service that the library provides.